GODDESS

Goddess

Stories

Emily Marcus Gong

BROKEN TRIBE PRESS

Published by Broken Tribe Press
Lawrence Landing Company
Raleigh, North Carolina 27609
United States of America
www.brokentribepress.com

Broken Tribe Press is a proud member of

Independent Book Publishers Association
 and
Community of Literary Magazines and Presses

CONTENTS

FORWARD

Despite the age-old wisdom to "write about what you know" or "what you don't know about what you know," I have always found that the easiest place to start any writing is with whatever is keeping me up at night. Stories have provided just enough distance from my anxieties to examine them with a looser grip, to explore the realm of possibilities with an openness that feels antithetical to the claustrophobic spirals of worry. Many of the stories in this collection grapple with the idea of motherhood, which makes sense—they were written during graduate school, a time when I wondered if I would ever be a mom, if I wanted to, what it would mean in terms of my identity if I were or were not to have kids. I dreamed and fantasized about small footprints in the sand and sharing my favorite songs with little humans that were undoubtedly mine. And at the same time a two-pronged terror constantly haunted me: that I was too anxious, too self-absorbed, too much of a mess to be a good mom. Thus, I might have kids and fail them, losing myself in the process. Or I might not have kids at all, not be able to have kids, never meet the right partner to have kids with, might not even want kids?

Call it fate, irony, or divine humor, but I found out this book would be published nearly five years after writing it while four months pregnant. Revisiting these stories through the editing process while pregnant and in the throes of postpartum, in addition to being a wild ride, has only expanded my awe at the power of myths, the very inspiration for this collection. There is certainly much value in retelling, but maybe even more in re-listening. What I heard when I read these self-titled "echoes," years after I had written them, was new, as I was a new version of myself. Through the lens of this raw, extreme moment of my life was a call to focus less on the story of my life and more on living. I saw my characters' terrors about their own identities, but also a beam of curiosity, of reframing the question of what they should be doing, feeling, or being among life's constant transitions to what possibilities could exist on the other side. Motherhood so far, i.e. life with my four-month-old son, is not something I ever could have imagined or pictured, and I doubt I will ever begin to pull apart how it fits into my identity, the sudden before and after of it, the moment-by-moment reshaping of it within my day let alone my life. The value of these stories lies less in any degree of "truth" they represent, even as fiction the beliefs and questions they wrestle with have already vanished or changed beyond recognition. Instead, their worth is in what a close friend dubbed the "unique alchemy," that is what you, my reader, create with them.

HUNTRESS

Every scent is an omen. We read the air and the trees, asking nature to pull us forward or send us home. The sun, finally sunk, inks out her last exuberant display on the dusted sky (one day I hope to be the type of person whose presence is still felt after she leaves a room). The bike path is nearly empty by the time we meet, our laden backpacks speaking mid-autumn myths of two middle-school girls heading off to finish projects and study sessions to the few passersby. When we return, empty-handed, it will be too dark to notice us, and the straggling post-dinner dog-walkers of this hour will be cozying up under fleece blankets with their husbands, while their dogs snore at their feet or in the crook of their knees. We take the familiar dirt offshoot, Tessa first, descending through the woods until we finally reach the water.

Tonight, the lake smells wholesome, its green is so deep and fresh I almost forget it's the same body of water as the putrid puddle of last July, when the rains stopped and the heat slurped up its coolness, the elementary school children filled it with urine, and dead trout cropped up along its circumference, dulling out from silver to grey to brown like everything else. That summer we traded out our afternoon swims for popsicles on the porch swing, followed by sprawling out on the cold tiled floor of my foyer, the A/C buzzing overhead while we shared our secret dreams for how different eighth grade would be from seventh. But that summer was centuries ago, before any of the sourness spread into our lives, before Tessa turned stony and quiet, and I'd be surprised if any drop of that lake remained in this new one, so pure, almost humming, filled with what can only be godliness. Like the lake, they say every cell in the human body is replaced every seven years, our lives are an endless gradual process of dying and rebirth. I wonder if tonight our rebirth will be immediate or completed only after every old cell has died and all new ones are born from the root of our devotion to the promise we are about to make. We reach the clearing and inhale the cool earthy air. The lake says yes for us, and that is enough.

***

I won't admit to my fiancé that the only reason I want to go to my ten-year high school reunion is to see if Tessa is there. Mostly, because I know she won't be. She detests this town, the people of this town I should say. Perhaps the landscape was enough to bring her back. I remember she used to ask how such beauty could be filled with such ugliness, an ugliness I never understood as a child, but looking back as a quasi-adult regret never asking her about.

In college we lost touch, though the drifting started in high school. You know how it goes. First, they track us into different courses. She was always smarter than me. She had that piercing brilliance about her, like she understood everything before it was even explained. I think she did. This was only confirmed when she opened her mouth, and out poured a whirling, enrapturing storm of history and art and logic and literature. It was like she had read every book in the world, ran it through a sieve to get the most striking parts out, and then wove the components together to make these astounding questions and observations. *Misogyny started when man named nature. You ever think that tears embody how sadness is the most productive emotion?* In my basic high school classes, I made a basic high school friend, a spike-your-hot-chocolate-before-the-football-game friend, a let's-go-to-the-mall-and-get-matching-thongs friend. And then I made another. By the end of my senior year, I was part of a basic-high-school-clique. They were light. We had crushes that we giggled at in the hallways, we went to parties, we debated the best technique for hand-jobs, got thrown out of movie theaters for tossing candy at the backs of people's heads, drove and drove around dark backroads far too fast. My times with Tessa got gloomier and gloomier, I tried to Jekyll-and-Hyde between who I was with her and who I was with them, but often failed. She couldn't hide her disappointment in me, and I couldn't deny how my times with her were racked with guilt and ickyness. I don't think I've ever quite forgiven myself for that sense of failure, which I used to think was a failure of simply not being good enough, smart enough, bold enough for her, but now I fear was a failure to name what I suspected had happened to her all along. As if uttering the words would somehow make me complicit.

The last time we hung out was on Thanksgiving break of our first year of college. We went for a walk. It was awkward. She was depressed at being home, claiming there was no one in the town who understood her, who she cared about. She said it to hurt me, but our friendship had fizzled to such an extent that it didn't. College had taken me so far away from her judgment, it had lost power over me. I remember vividly, changing the subject, asking her about her school friends, surely she had met more worthy people at the Ivy league school, people who she cared about. Anything to change the topic and go home. To my relief she nodded, saying she and all of her suitemates had joined the feminist group on campus. It was a moment of relief, I could picture her staying up late and hashing out lofty ideas, marching through campus with her tribe of fellow intellectuals. She ended up on the right path for her, and so everything worked out how it was supposed to. Then she turned to me, with an unblinking, icy look, sinking the dagger, "Yeah, everyone is fine. I mean, at least, they seem to stick to their word."

10 years later and the words still sting, though with the bite of inferiority– I was never quite on her level– or the guilt of not keeping the promise, of not asking why we made the promise in the first place, I am not sure. Maybe after all this time, I just want to know that she did do OK. That my suspicions about that ritual we performed were simply my overactive imagination paired with our trauma-obsessed generation. Or maybe I just want to know what she did next, having heard only whispers here and there. Luke sneaks up behind me in the mirror where I am shimmying the mascara through my lashes. He plants a kiss on my cheek and slings his arms around me. I know what's coming next.

"Do we really need to go?" He asks our reflection in the mirror.

"I just want to make an appearance. I gotta show off this rock somewhere." I look at the neat cushion-cut diamond he gave me a month ago. He laughs, kisses my cheek again, and goes to the closet to pick a shirt. He's not one to put up a fight. He holds up two shirts, one light blue, one white. Turns to me for approval, asks, "Hey, you think that freaky friend of yours is gonna be there?"

***

In this dusky hour we can just make out the five half-submerged rocks we need to traverse to reach the island. We know them so well we could cross without a flashlight but use them anyway, knowing any fumble would send us right home. Tessa goes first like always and reaches out her hand when it's my turn to take the biggest step between the third and fourth rocks. I'm surprised by the clamminess of her palm, but I can feel her steadiness regardless. We've always been best friends, but tonight we will become sisters. We reach the other side easily, silently, and make our way through the few balding trees to the table. The table is a rectangular, speckled boulder with a top flat enough for picnics or card games. We unroll our towels on the damp ground across from each other and sit. I want to ask Tessa so badly if she is scared, if she is sure, but we promised each other we would only speak after the oath has been uttered.

We begin. Tessa unzips her backpack and takes out a stuffed bear I recognize from the pile of pillows on her bed. She puts him on the altar. My turn. I start with the largest object, my American Girl Doll, Samantha, and place her beside the bear. A pink tutu. A ratty white blanket. Feathered boas. Colored chalk. Barbies. Slinkys. Plastic food. Gel pens. Barrettes with bows. Tiaras.

Glitter. Flavored lip gloss. Temporary tattoos. A jump rope. Teen magazines. Cat ears. A magic wand. Bottles of bubbles. Nail polish. Training bras.

By the time we finish laying everything out, it's nighttime and cloudless. We make our way to the other side of the island, where we can see you, the moon, which we know will be full. The moon is even fuller and more shocking than we could have imagined, and she licks a milky path along the water's surface, she fills us with an ancient determination.

***

Luke and I enter the same dive bar they held our five-year high school reunion, and I realize it's the same exact crowd who was here five years ago: the athletes and the superlatives. Back then I was still very close with my clique. We all went together, not even a year out from college, none of us had accomplished much of note. All our job titles ended with assistant. The majority of us couldn't afford our own places so we were back in our childhood rooms. Then we had stayed for only an hour, enough time to scout out who had peaked in high school, but everyone looked the exact same. These past five years were different, longer somehow even though everyone claims time starts to move more quickly. I knew others would be engaged too, some already married with kids. It feels validating to know that for all the spiraling and indecisions of my twenties, the mindless jobs and wretched situationships, I am finally doing something concretely adult, I am getting married. Before we approach the cordoned off area, I send a text to the group,

"You guys here yet?" I know at least a few of them are going to stop by. Sensing my sudden anxiety, Luke goes to grab beers for us.

I recognize the girl who came after me alphabetically. She was always nice. Every time we were paired together for labs or projects we would go to her enormous house, where her family had a secondary living room they called a sitting room. Her mom would make us popcorn or hot chocolate. We were never friends but could have been. We hug and start in on the 10 years of updates. She introduces her girlfriend whom she lives with in the city, and Luke is his normal friendly and inquisitive self. He asks questions about their jobs and pets and apartment. Sometimes I wonder if he would be called abrasive if he was a woman. Everyone adores him. Soon a few members of the old clique show up, and the tension I felt earlier dissipates. It was the right decision to come. We knock back drinks and reflect on our old antics. The easing of my nerves and drunkenness compound and I am vaguely happy and bored, though some neuron still clings onto the hope that there will be news of Tessa. Deep down, I want her to see that this path has been the right one for me, as completely opposite as it may be from the one we envisioned for us both on that weird night in the woods so many years ago. I ask the crowd, "Hey has anyone heard anything about Tessa Reynolds?"

Everyone turns to me.

"Weren't you two close?"

I shrug, "Sort of. But we lost touch after graduation."

"I think I heard she was moving to Canada."

"My mom ran into her mom. Mentioned something about her being a journalist or something. I guess she uses a pen name though. Won't even tell her own family what she writes."

"You think it's like hard core erotica?"

I shake my head, laugh at the thought. "No way."

"If you want to know so badly, why don't you just text her?"

What's the harm? She's probably changed her number anyway. I type it out and show it to Luke, while the rest of the group goes on to talk about that time we stole all of the traffic cones in our town and blocked off roads for fun, laughing hysterically as people slowly pulled their cars up and turned around to take a different street.

Hey Tessa, I know it's been forever, but I'm in town for Thanksgiving and just stopped by the reunion. Any chance you're coming?

Before I even slip my phone back into my purse it dings. I'm expecting a confused "who's this?" or a "sorry but this number is no longer in service" message, but it's her. The rest of the group has already lost interest. I read the text in shock.

Hey, good to hear from you. I am here for the holiday, too. Wasn't planning on it, but would love to see you. I'll come say hi, where at?

***

Drenched in moonlight, we begin the second part of the ritual. Tessa turns first towards the moon, and I stand directly behind her. Sliding an elastic from her wrist, she makes a low ponytail right at her hairline. I wish I could see through her head to know what her face was saying. Her hair, blue-black and silken, is the exact opposite of mine. I take the dark tail in my left hand and the scissors in my right. I search the back of Tessa for any sign of emotion, wait for her to turn and yell stop, but even her hands are relaxed, hanging gently at her sides. I hear her voice in my head, *Come on, I am ready. We're ready. We have to do this.* She's been so down lately, it's almost started to scare me. I know this is the only way to bring her back to her old self, it's all she's talked about for weeks. I begin working the scissors through. Her hair is thicker than expected and it takes a solid ten seconds of work to cut the ponytail fully off. As she turns around, I expect to see tears and solemness. Instead, she is exuberant, her hair falls to her ears, her eyes are wild with liberation. We switch, and something in my chest collapses. As slowly as possible, I wrangle my frizzy mane into a ponytail. I remind myself *this is what I want.* A lifetime of protection, of freedom and sisterhood. Just like Tessa said. I try not to let any of the tears slip over my eyelids, I want to be as strong as Tessa. So I look to the moon, and before I know it I feel the weight drop from my head. I turn to see Tessa beaming, holding my messy brown tress. Reaching up to feel where my hair ends, my new head feels buoyant, and I can't help but laugh out, the tears successfully escaping down my cheeks. Tessa laughs too, and we hug, still holding each other's amputated ponytails. After a moment the hug turns solemn, Tessa takes out the flashlight and we walk back to the altar. We add the ponytails to the pile and sit across from one another again. Joining hands we count to three, before uttering our vow.

***

The door opens across the room, and I know it's her. The crowd has already started to thin, and no one else would be arriving so late. I step outside the group to greet her. She is stunning. The thick black hair I severed years ago frames her angular face in a blunt bob. It shines like a pane of glass, and just brushes her severe collar bones. The brilliance in her face is still there, though more adult. Whereas before it combined with a youthful earnestness to learn, there is none of that now. This is a face that knows something, maybe everything, you don't. The deep red bordering purple lip stain professionally lines her cupid's bow lips and dances against her warm ivory skin. I don't need to talk to her to know she has made it. She emanates success, a fire ignited, wild and aroar.

We barely get the chance to hug and say hello before the group is around us again. Moths always flock to a flame. She greets everyone in our circle, people she barely knew and somewhat despised, shakes hands with their plus-ones, and then I introduce her to Luke. I see the slightest twitch of emotion on her face at the word fiancé. It's so miniscule I may have projected it, thinking her the same girl she was at 14 who hated boys with a piercing, persistent vengeance. Again, the guilt comes, an instinct that I should have recognized something was wrong, that something had happened. I think back to that summer, before ninth grade at the lake, I was so enthralled in the mystic game we played, the ritual, I wasn't too young to know that my friend was trying to tell me something.

"Congratulations!" She says to me. Her smile is a blank, icy sheath that is dazzling but lifeless. She has asked everyone what they're up to, but somehow avoided revealing a glimmer into her elusive life.

"But what about YOU?" I ask, reflecting back that fakeness in a sing-songy way that makes me at once feel like an aunt and want to shrivel up and die. I tone it down, "What have you been up to in the last, uh, decade?"

She laughs. "I actually, well, for starters I live in Vermont now."

"And we hear you're like a famous reporter or something?" Someone pipes in. I realize that everyone is waiting for her response. I feel validated. Like maybe everyone forgot just how destined for greatness she always was except for me. It's like a twisted version of I told you so.

"A journalist?" she smirks, confused. "Where did you hear that?" She displays not an ounce of hubris for being, so evidently, the talk of the town.

"Well, my mom saw your mom downtown maybe a month ago and—" I feel bad for the girl who has to admit she still keeps an ear to the gossip of the town, we all do, but she got herself caught in the crosshairs of this one.

"Ha, my mom and her exaggerations." She shakes her head. "I wrote a couple op-eds for the local paper. Just some thoughts on the election. I'm actually a financial consultant." She looks me dead in the eye.

Without saying verbally, "oh that's boring," the group manages to communicate that by mechanically chirping out the appropriate follow-up questions and then turning the conversation to my upcoming wedding. Luke takes over, because I am distracted. A thousand conversations ring in my head about our dream jobs. There's no way she's in finance, she detested talking about money, let alone dealing with it. I try to shake it off, this feeling that she is playing us all, me particularly, while muttering out details about honeymoon ideas and venues and stupid signature cocktails. *Why did she come here? What does she want me to know?* I am relieved when people start making excuses to leave. I need to talk to her alone. I tell Luke to wait at the car, he is drunk and even more obedient than usual.

"Did you drive here?" I ask as we gather our coats, knowing her parents' house is only about a 15-minute walk away. She smiles.

"No," she said. "Still taking our old bike path."

"You want us to drop you off? I swear I sobered up hours ago," I sound like I am still in high school.

"That's OK, you know I like to walk." I do know that.

We step out into the freezing November night. Without thinking, I start walking with her down the dark path. I don't know what comes over me, or us for that matter, but it's like there's a magnet pulling us to our offshoot, to the lake which sits halfway between downtown and her home. Meanwhile, we reflect on the evening, on where everyone ended up, what they ended up doing with their 20s. When we get to the offshoot, she goes first, but doesn't turn to make sure I make it down OK. We are not friends. We sit at the edge of the lake, it's too dark to traverse the rocks, and we look out on the island where we cut off each other's hair half our lifetime ago. This place is somehow still ours, though when I look her dead in the eye, I realize I don't know anything about the woman looking back at me.

"Finance?" I ask her, unable to maintain this façade.

She shakes her head and chuckles, "You of all people should know that people change." The remark comes off less petty than clever, but I can tell she still resents me.

"Maybe people just grow up," I manage to mumble.

She ponders this for a second, and I am reminded of the gloominess I felt around her in high school. "Have you?" She asks me. Her face is sincere and earnest, but the question still feels like a test.

"Grown up?" I ask, she nods. "I'm not sure. I don't think it's like a switch that goes off, you know? Maybe I have partially grown up."

She looks at her feet. She doesn't say anything, but for the first time the whole evening, I can guess what she's thinking. That for some people, it *is* like a switch, growing up is in someone else's control and abrupt. An entire world illuminated or cast in darkness in an instant. I look at the island. I am filled with grief and guilt for the friend I never was. I don't know what to say, what is there to say? When I look back the moon bounces off her face, and I am overcome with the sense that she may in fact have done what she said she would all along.

"Hey, remember that weirdo promise we made here as kids?" I laugh, trying to lighten the weight of the question I am about to ask, a weight that has made a home for itself in my chest all night, and if I am being honest, for years before this night. "You didn't keep it, did you?"

She looks at me without hesitation. "Yes," she says, matter of fact. "I did."

The word travels from my ears to my throat to my stomach. I know it's true, just like I knew it was true for her then. She had kept a promise we made as teens, so she would always keep it. *Who are you?* I want to ask her so badly, *how did you do it? What else have you done?*

"I'm sorry." It's all I can manage to say.

"It's in the past," she says, cold again, matter of fact.

"I've made my peace with it."

The word peace from her mouth shocks me. I realize it's because there is nothing peaceful about her presence. She is a woman filled with rage who once was a girl filled with rage. She was always too extreme for me, though we both wanted to think otherwise. She has not made her peace, because peace is something she would never accept. Peace isn't good enough. It occurs to me I might be the only person in the world who understands that.

We sit there in silence until my phone goes off. It's Luke asking me where I am. It breaks the spell that brought us here, and we begin our way back to the path. As we hug goodbye, I get the sense that this is the last time I will ever see her. After my apology, there is nothing left for us to say to each other. But the mystery of who she is now remains. *Was that why she came here?* I wonder, still puzzled by the unfolding of events that led us here. *Did she really need that closure?*

Before she turns the other way down the path, she reaches in her bag and hands me a package. She pats me on the arm, tells me to wait until I'm home, and disappears into the dark. From the weight and size, I know it's a book. *Why did she come tonight?* She has answered.

***

DIANA, GODDESS OF THE MOON, OF THE HUNT, OF THE WOODLAND. PROTECTRESS OF WOMEN, MOTHERS, AND VIRGINS: TONIGHT WE JOIN YOU IN SISTERHOOD. WE OFFER OUR CHILDHOOD AND PROMISE OUR CELIBACY FOREVER. PROTECT OUR CHASTITY AND WE WILL HONOR YOU WITH OUR

PURITY UNTIL DEATH. LET US JOIN YOU IN THE ETERNAL HUNT, SO THAT WE OURSELVES MIGHT NEVER BE HUNTED AGAIN.

****

I tear the packaging off in the front seat of the car. Luke is leaning against the window almost asleep. On the back cover of the book reads the same words we yelled out into the moon more than 14 years ago, and my stomach drops. I flip it over to see the godforsaken title: *Huntress*. The news clips from a few years ago about a novel I deemed too gory to read flash through my mind. At first, they were innocent: *Self-Published Horror Novel Breaks Records, Named "NYT Best Seller," Hunting the Huntress: Fans Speculate Over Identity of Diana Venatrix.* And then the rest: *Series of Gruesome Castrations Linked to NYT Best Seller "Huntress". Victims Come Forward, Claim Novel Covered "Intimate" Details of their Former Castrations. Why No one will Ever Find Diana Venatrix. The Venatrix Paradox: Why Would She Write It?*

I was the only person in the world who would know the answer to that question.

Because she was already used to being prey, because she could never accept peace, because celibacy wasn't enough, because she was a protectress of women, mothers, and virgins, because she needed her message to be heard far and wide: LET THE ETERNAL HUNT BEGIN.

THE GOOD GODDESS

The hot Roman sun is formidable even in May. It cooks the sidewalks, the ruins, all seven hills, the vespas, the trains. I hate David for making us walk to Piramide, but I don't want to start the conference off as a bad sport. Soon after crossing the Tiber I see the ancient tomb in the distance and feel my rage cool to a simmer. It always surprises me how few people seem even to notice the ancient pyramid smack in the center of the city while thousands continue to shit themselves at Giza. To be fair, the Pyramid of Caius Cestius is only ¼ as high as the great pyramids, but still size isn't everything, right?

"Laurie! Pick it up, the train leaves in seven!"

This time it's fucking Gary. I should have splurged and booked my own hotel for the week, but the university insists on making all of our travel arrangements for funded conferences. I know I should be grateful they humored me with the early flight and even paid for all three of us to go, as we are all well aware, I would have been the first on the chopping block. David, the historian, and Gary, the archaeologist, were guaranteed spots. Then it was between me, the art historian, and Jane, the philologist. It's the first trip I've made without my husband and children in over fifteen years. As infants I couldn't fathom leaving them for more than a few hours, and then there was always a birthday or a play or a final swimming meet, and soon the opportunities to travel just stopped presenting themselves. But when Jane's recent hip surgery prevented her from making the trek, I decided to make my case based on my expertise in Augustan-age frescos, two of which had been recently uncovered at the site.

I'm excited, this conference is the first of its kind. Before the site is opened to the public, the university leading the dig is holding this "open-air" symposium, bringing researchers from all facets and all corners of the world, in hopes the event would spark new, innovative, and interdisciplinary lines of research. Each day will involve guided tours followed by breakout discussion groups based on subject area and research interests. I wonder if the idea will backfire, all hopes of collaboration extinguished by the aggressive gust of competition.

On the train, I watch the dense, graffiti-covered buildings thin out, soon replaced by the lush Italian landscape. When we arrive here in Ostia Antica, just a few miles from the coast, the air is still sweaty and heavy. In the near distance I see the familiar ruins of the ancient port city. I remember the first time I came here, on my study abroad dozens of years ago. After spending weeks in the Roman forum, maneuvering through crowds of tourists while our professors bellowed out lessons, Ostia was a reprieve, an entire ancient port city to ourselves. Our professors led us around the forum, the stunning mosaics, and the massive amphitheater. They explained that the whole Western part of the site had yet to be uncovered. While Mussolini had rushed as much of the excavations in the late 30s as possible, some valiant archaeologists had protected a large western area for future archaeologists, knowing that they couldn't predict how much technology would evolve. Some secrets they weren't prepared to unearth. After our lectures all those years ago they let us wander. It was our playground; 35 classics nerds playing "forum," giving orations on the rostrum, climbing atop column bases, acting out Senecan tragedies in the theater. I imagine that limby, naive college student I was, gazing out over those thousands-year-old ruins and picturing the life of an academic, jetting from one ancient site to the next, hosting spirited dinner parties where guests knew far too much about the wine, an oak-filled home library with a collection of rare books, endless hunger for research, even fame. What would she think of me now, hanging onto tenure by a thread, the spark for new ideas slowly extinguished by the constant brain-noise of being a mom, of the have-you-seen-my-[insert object, normally phone]s and what-time-was-that-[insert activity]s. Approaching the ruins this time, it feels like a different kind of playground, dozens of grey-haired professors, flocking to see exactly what that elusive "future archaeology" has uncovered.

We gather in the amphitheater for opening remarks, where the lead archaeologists remind us of all their exciting discoveries in the last five years of excavations, as if everyone in the audience wasn't following the news of their work religiously. Seven new buildings: a mammoth bath complex, three private residences, a small insula, a warehouse, and a small temple to Bona Dea, the "Good Goddess," a figure whose ambiguity has always piqued my curiosity. Nevertheless, we clap enthusiastically at their pronouncements and exchange excited glances with each other. For tours we're split up into groups based on language. There are English, German, and Italian guides. Gary makes a big show of deciding whether or not to go in an English or German group, whoop-dee-doo. Ultimately, he decides he should stick with us and we are joined by an archaeologist from the UK, two historians from UGA, and a mysterious medievalist from Illinois. Our guide is a peppy PhD from Sapienza whose main job is to keep us on a tight schedule moving from one site to the next.

The tour is a whirlwind, we breeze from one site to the next, everyone explains everything to each other, "Oh this must have been some sort of water feature." "This must date to the first century B.C." "Isn't it odd that the portico has six columns?" "Notice the orthogonal plan." Gary and David twitter at each other like tweens. The historians take copious notes, and the guide gets more and more frustrated trying to get them to move along. I snap photos of a few details, a particularly ornate Corinthian column head, a delightful mosaic in the courtyard of one of the private residences. We all signed waivers that we wouldn't post any pictures until the site opens to the public next spring. I try to hide my impatience to get to the frescoes.

Our group is the last to see the Temple of Bona Dea. The walls come up just over my head, the brick pattern consistent with a 1st C BC date. Unlike most Roman temples, this one is walled. It's a maze of small rooms, and it's hard not to get lost wandering from one cubby to the next. There are at least eleven rooms; some lead to dead ends. The place still echoes with privacy, secrecy. This is where women would've come for healing. The one place where men weren't allowed. For some reason, I think of the locker room at the Jewish Community Center back home, the cubbies of lockers and the mystical healing qualities of the sauna. Maybe our good goddess is our aging, resilient bodies, maybe it always was.

At last, I reach the frescoes, side by side. This must have been the *cella*, where women brought their offerings to the mysterious goddess. Not much is known about Bona Dea, because women were not taught to write, and the male historian's accounts are more speculative than anything. She is, in a way, a conflation of all other goddesses, what's left when you strip back their unique attributes: chastity, motherhood, witch. The left fresco is a typical Augustan period decoration, like the fashionable wallpaper of the time, a red wall punctuated by ornate columns and windows opening up to scenes of fruit trees and birds. It reminds me of so many other frescoes I've studied before that my brain blares with all the connections. No matter how many times I see this scene, I always think it weird that walls were painted to look like windows, the very thing they are not.

The fresco on the right shakes me. Bona Dea sits on a yellow throne, clad in a flowing white chiton. In her left arm, she holds a cornucopia, overflowing with fruit and grain. A serpent winds its way around her right arm so that her hand is level with the snake's head, both reaching out to you. Bona Dea is the epitome of every ancient goddess I have ever seen, beautiful, pure, sexy, maternal, her expression calm and reassuring, yet knowing. She has the power to nurture and the power to heal. The snake as a symbol of healing always gets me, I trip on the associations with Eden, evil, seduction, and temptation. Bona Dea is the ultimate woman, an abstraction, an amalgamation. I think of my daughters back home, 16 and 12, and the girl-women they idolize, their faces blurred by filters and their personalities watered down to please the masses. Who have I taught them to be? What have I taught them to tame? I think of myself and the sacrifices I've made to be a good wife, a good mom, a good woman. Had motherhood really watered me down, or had it just nurtured a different part of myself that was there all along, and so what if that part fit more neatly into society's expectations of me?

Next to me I see the medievalist draw up a quick sketch, and soon we are joined by Gary and David. Before long, the historians are there too, and then the whole group is packed into the small chamber. The pairs whisper to each other about their observations, the symbols and style, the expression. Only then does it occur to me that I am one of two women in the room, just me and the medievalist, and we are the only people with our mouths shut. The historians bumble on about the scandalous rituals that honored Bona Dea that men were not invited to, the drinking, the bloody sacrifices. They sound like middle school boys hypothesizing about what happens at an all-girl sleepover.

"I mean this was just an evolution of the Thesmophoria, your textbook fertility festival. The snake as phallus, the cornucopia as children, I mean it's the same thing."

"I wouldn't conflate the two so much, I mean of course, curiously, these traditions persist, but if Bona Dea's was a harvest festival, it wouldn't have happened in May."

For the first time I realize that it's May now, the organizers must have timed the conference for that reason. Or maybe it was a coincidence.

"Well that makes perfect sense. A festival at the beginning of growing season. I mean every fertility festival was always also about a fertile harvest, don't you agree?"

I hear his words, but I also hear something more sinister.

I think about what I remember of the Thesmophoria, the women departing the polis to complete their witchy rituals burying pig carcasses in the ground. Pigs, the wildest of the domesticated animals, except for women.

The archaeologist pipes in, citing Juvenal, about how by the 2nd century the festival was a massive drunk sexual-free-for-all, open to all castes of women and men dressed in drag. Gary and David banter in the corner about how involved men must have been to pay for and erect such a shrine. Eventually all topics of conversation turn to the heat, and one by one the academics begin to leave the room, last in, first out.

When it's just the two of us women left, the release of body heat feels like a breeze, and I notice that the medievalist picks up her pencil to finish her sketch, clearly as distracted as I was by the conversation. I remember my camera, the strap at my neck now slicked with sweat from the day of walking with barely any coverage from the sun (not a lot of roofs made it past antiquity). I want to say something to her, to make some remark about the commentary we just heard, but I don't want to ruin her focus again. I lift my camera, aiming directly at the goddess.

Through my viewfinder, I see it, unmistakably, I see it: the serpent flicks its tongue. It all happens in an instant. The goddess turns her face to mine, she wants an offering. I drop my camera and it clangs heavy against my chest, throwing me back a few steps. I turn to look at the medievalist, and realize, I am alone.

***

Back in my room, I can finally collect myself. I am a big girl, used to pulling myself together and holding back emotions until I am alone. I've fought tears back into my eyeballs more times than I'd care to admit, though this is just what it means to be a woman. She can be diminished, unmoored, or gutted, and still, hold it in. A revolution can occur inside of her, and she won't flinch. I don't know if it's our natural power to bear entire realities within ourselves or a trauma response from our domestication. My world just turned on its axis, but I can still wait until I get to my hotel room to freak out.

I run through it a million times, the flick of the tongue, the goddess. She didn't say it, but I heard her demand for an offering. I consider whether I should call my husband to tell him I'm on my way to the hospital because I had a hallucination caused by heatstroke. He'd be worried, but he at least wouldn't worry the kids. But every time I pick up the phone, I calm myself, I feel fine, it's just your wacky imagination. Maybe you didn't see it at all.

That night I dream of snakes. I don't exactly see them, but I know they are there. I sense them. The room is full of snakes, yellow and black bodies in heaving, living masses, swirling, and whispering, and hushing. They are everything holy and evil in the world, terrifying and good, they lure me and disgust me, they are everything I have ever been and everything I am not, they are Bona Dea and mother nature, my daughters, me, they are everything we love about women and everything that makes us recoil, I want to control them and to own them and to toss them to the wild that they are.

I wake around 3 and find solace the only way I know how, through google. I search Bona Dea + snakes, Bona

Dea + offering, and I find all the information I already knew. I think back to the fresco, the way the first one looked just like a dozen frescoes I'd seen before, and the way the goddess herself blended into about every ancient goddess I have ever known: Ops, Terra, even Venus. I try something else, I remove Bona Dea from my search. A name immediately emerges that seems vaguely familiar: Angizia. It resounds with a hiss in my ears, I am satisfied for tonight. I sleep again and dream of nothing.

***

It takes me until the last day of the conference to muster up enough humility to ask David what he knows about Angizia. Apart from surface level info, I don't trust the internet. The sites on Angizia seem witchy and unreliable. I sit next to him on the train while he man-spreads. I know the best course of action is to ask abruptly and without flattery.

"David, what can you tell me about Angizia?"

"The snake goddess?" He's reliable, I have to give it to him.

"Yep."

"What about her? I don't know much." I know this is the predecessor to him knowing a whole lot. He spends the rest of the ride explaining the whole story, paying particular attention to the cult festival that honored her in pagan times.

"It evolved into a Catholic festival, of course, the Festi dei Serpari." There's that ridiculous Italian accent I was dreading. "I think it happens right about this time of year, in a small town in Abruzzo."

I feel like that's a hint. Bona Dea's festival and Angizia's falling around the same time, the connection to serpents. We step back out into the ruins, which have never felt more alive.

Later on, I see that the festival is happening in a week. I don't think. I book the only place I can find in the area, I'll work the details out later.

***

The train stop in Sulmona is peaceful and quiet this early in the morning. I, as per usual, doubt that I am at the right station, on the right track, going the right direction. I have 20 minutes to rest, freak out, and confirm with someone that this is the train that will take me to Cocullo. I see a young woman ambling towards my track, and as she passes me in the instant our eyes meet, I point at the train and ask "Cocullo?" She nods. I know I should practice my Italian. After her confirmation, I confirm again with the attendant as I board.

The train lurches forward and starts creeping out of the station, the gears whirling and churning underfoot. Soon the sky is whipping past, and then it's syncopated with blotches of green. I wish the ride was longer. I could so easily doze off with the soft light pouring in between the trees, medieval towns occasionally rising in the distance. We pull into the station, and from my seat I can see the hilltop town rising above me. I start gathering my bags.

"No no no!" The young woman from the station calls out to me, she has been sitting behind me the whole time. "Goriano Sicoli not Cocullo."

I look at the sign outside that she is pointing to which reads "Goriano" and sink back to my seat embarrassed. I turn around to the woman to say thank you. "Too early for travel," I joke.

"It's the next stop." She laughs. "You are here visiting Abruzzo for the first time?"

"I was in Sulmona a couple of times, but this is my first time going to Cocullo."

"Going for the Festi dei Serpari?"

I nod. "I hear it's quite the sight!"

She shakes her head. "I have never been. I hate snakes."

"They are not my favorite either."

She gives me a surprised look. "No?"

"Not really. But work brought me to Italy, I had a conference last week, and I saw that this was happening and figured I would be silly to miss it." She still looks skeptical, so I keep explaining. "Besides, I wanted another excuse to come back to Abruzzo, Sulmona is one of my favorite places."

"Is that so? You know we rarely get many tourists there, it's where my family is from. Just lots of people for the jazz festival, then quiet the rest of the year."

I tell her about my first trip to Sulmona, when I was 22 and celebrating my college graduation with my first solo trip to Europe. Of course, the birthplace of my favorite Roman poet (Ovid, duh) was on my map, and I fell in love with the town's spirit. Since that trip, I have used many excuses to revisit the town. I even managed to sneak in a night there between the conference and the festival. I am frankly shocked that the university let me trade out my return ticket, but I guess when they don't have to spend more money, they can be generous in spirit.

"Really," she encourages me, "why do you want to see the snake festival so badly?"

I don't blame her for being curious. A middle-aged woman headed to a town full of snakes, just for kicks doesn't make sense. "So I am in Italy studying this very mysterious goddess called Bona Dea, a new fresco of her has just been discovered." She nods, urging me on. "And I just have this weird feeling that she may be connected to this place or this ritual, maybe at least to Angizia in some way." I don't want to assume she knows or doesn't know who Angizia is.

"Angizia?"

"She was this ancient snake goddess, her cult lived around here. And I guess the festival has roots in an ancient rite involving her."

"And you think she has something to do with this, Bona Dea?" She asks me sincerely, curious in a way that I know my colleagues would never be.

"I do." The train starts pulling into what actually is Cocullo this time. We wish each other well and I make my way to the Airbnb, which was the only available one within miles of the area. There are no hotels in Cocullo. It's late in the afternoon, and the village is smaller than I expected and already buzzing with activity, even a day before the festival. Tucked into the Peligna valley, the mountains curve around it in a way that feels nestled, safe. The buildings are a combination of muted oranges, beiges, and whites and they slope up towards the town square and church beyond. I reach the door of a two-story old apartment building, wildly close to the main piazza, and ring the buzzer as instructed. After a moment, a young couple from Trieste greets me excitedly, whisking my bags off to my room and setting the Moka pot on the stove. They've even printed a small map for me and marked it by hand. After we exchange pleasantries and small talk, they dive into the main event. It occurs to me that I know so little about the town and the modern festival I will be attending tomorrow, only that it entails marching a statue of the town's Patron Saint, San Domenico, covered in live snakes through the streets.

"Tomorrow is going to be madness here," the husband, Luca, explains. "The traffic today is not even close to what it will be like tomorrow."

"Really?"

"Oh completely! You saw it's just like one road to get from Anversa, that road will be completely blocked for miles and miles."

"Well, I am lucky I was able to stay tonight. Are there any other people renting out their homes?"

"This is not our home," Luca says.

"I mean your mother's home, right?"

This time Julia explains, "My mother lives a couple hours from here. A very distant relative lived here, but now we just use it during festival season."

"Oh, I understand," I nod.

"Yes, so only about 400 people live in this town."

"Just 400?" I have taught lectures nearly that size.

"Yes, and only 100 of those people live all year, the winter is nearly inhabitable here because the roads are blocked with snow."

"I would have never guessed from how lively it is today."

"Well festival season is a different story. I think the reason the tradition is so important is partly because it is so isolated throughout the year, tradition can last longer you know?"

I imagine the surrounding hills and mountains, protectors of more than just land.

"So what's the best plan for tomorrow? Should I start in the square or—"

"There is not a large territory to traverse. Just walk out and you will see the snakes. Follow the crowds."

This is so typical Laurie, my anxiety about arriving here is immediately replaced with terror about what I signed up for. Travel anxiety can be a great distraction. "Are they, um, just out there?"

"Oh no, they are all with the Serpari, the catchers. See the charmers get paid for their snakes, by the town." Luca explains. "But all the snakes they bring are harmless."

I nod, not fully comforted. Back in my room I watch YouTube videos of the festival from last year to put my mind at ease, but they are all too shaky or distant to instill any calm. I FaceTime my daughters. My husband picks up the phone at such an unflattering angle, too close and below the chin, I question my attraction for him. Repulsion is not as far from attraction as one would think. He hands the phone off, because the young one, Jessie, is itching to describe in detail everything they've eaten in the last 24 hours since we talked. She asks me to do the same, and I leave out the gelato, because that just seems cruel. In the background her older sister, Michelle, smiles at her sister's intricate critique of the stir-fry Adam made for them the previous night (the toasted sesame seeds were a nice touch, but he should have used fresh veggies instead of frozen, or at least boiled the frozen veggies first, rookie mistake). We are a food family. Before hanging up, Michelle says she misses me, which fills me with warmth and worry at the same time, she doesn't normally admit that. I bury my *is she OK* and *am I a terrible mother* in a pile of research, two gooey arancini from the food stall in the piazza, and a generous glass of Montepulciano before passing out.

In the morning, I am woken up by the clamor of people just as the sun comes up. I go downstairs to find that Luca and Julia have already left for the day. There is a croissant waiting for me, which I inhale on the way out the door. I don't want to miss anything. The main road is already bustling, and the crowd continues to thicken throughout the morning, food stalls line it as far as I can see selling preserved fish, cheese, and cured meats, and soon the streets are filled with music; the church bells constantly sing. I start moving with the crowd towards the main piazza, and the energy is exuberant, people shake my hand and sing. I am reminded of how little Americans know how to celebrate as a community, festivals are just not the same. A snake charmer puts on a show, somehow holding 10 coiling snakes in his two knotted hands. When I make it to the main piazza, I see people holding canvas bags, tins, and boxes of every material. It takes me another moment to realize they are all filled with snakes. People show them off to passersby and friends, their yellow and black bodies unravelling from within. Oddly, I feel calm amidst the pandemonium, these people know how to interact with the animals. These are not the snakes of my nightmares.

In an Italian crowd there is no such thing as walking,

you just move, becoming a part of the rolling body of one. As I near the small sanctuary of San Domenico, I am shuffled down a dark passage. Within I see the statue of the saint, the main attraction of the day. He looks like a big plastic doll. I also see people within the sanctuary, collecting fistfuls of white dirt. I muster up the courage to ask the family near me what they're doing, using my pieced together Italian.

They tell me that they are collecting dirt to ward off snakes. *Ward off the snakes? Didn't they just bring all these snakes into the town?* I am so overwhelmed trying to understand this festival. After some back and forth in my terrible Italian, I start to think that this festival is more about warding off evil than about the peoples' relationship with their environment. I watch as each member of the family kisses the molar of the saint and rings a small bell with their teeth, and others around do the same. Suddenly everyone is encouraging me to take a turn, explaining that this will protect me from toothaches for a year. I am disgusted but do it anyway. I hate disappointing people, even strangers.

Soon I am shuffled away from the sanctuary, and I begin to make my way back to the Airbnb. As instructed, I should be back to the balcony by 11 a.m. for the procession. As my hosts explained, it's not the best view, the piazza is distant but visible, but it is surely better than watching from the crowd. When I get there, the couple waits for me with a gorgeous antipasto spread.

"You made it at the perfect moment," Julia announces, kissing me on one cheek and then the other. Luca does the same.

"Wow, you didn't have to do all this."

"We would be greedy not to share this view."

I want to ask them so much more about everything I just saw, the red dots on some of the snakes, the women in what must be traditional dresses, but I feel like I am imposing enough.

"He should come out any moment now."

"The priest?"

They nod.

Within seconds he emerges from the sanctuary, encouraging people to move back and make room. He is followed by a procession of two women balancing enormous hats on their heads though I can't make out exactly what they resemble. I note it down to google later. Following the women, the band starts up, and behind them I can see the plastic looking statue of the Saint. He is carried by four men, who put him down just outside of the sanctuary. Julia turns to me and explains that the Serpari are placing the chosen snakes at that moment. When they raise the saint again he is no longer a plastic dead thing, he is alive, completely encased in a mountain of snakes, all writhing and wriggling from his neck, head, shoulders, torso. Even from the distant balcony I can see them coil, threatening to drop into the crowd.

"If they fall off it's considered bad luck," says Luca completely engrossed in the sight. "But by the end of the whole parade, some have always fallen."

The procession makes its slow crawl down the main road. As it passes the balcony, I am mesmerized by the way they writhe and twist together. Three stories up, I can almost make out the flicks of their tongues. I can't get the image of Bona Dea's serpent out of my head, the flick of her tongue, the distinct feeling that the goddess wanted something from me. Among the heaving mass, the serene, powerful gaze of the saint is steady and calm, he is the protector. It occurs to me that the parade moves snake-like through the streets, winding and slithering through the small alleys of the town. It comes back around, again passing the balcony, and I can see that a few snakes have fallen.

"What happens to the fallen ones?" I ask Luca.

"People pick them up. At the end they're all released into the wild, but I know some try to keep them as pets."

"Brave souls."

"Yes, well, they are all supposed to be harmless. They remove the fangs or something, but I guess some of the charmers still get bitten quite often."

Soon the fireworks start, and I can't help but feel an overwhelming sense of confusion. Is this a celebration of snakes? Of man's power over snakes? Of the saint? Of an ancient goddess? Maybe it is too American to try and find an answer to this, but I decide to ask anyway.

"So I am a bit confused."

"It is a very mysterious event," says Julia. Luca has gone in to get the wine.

"I understand it is for the Saint, who protected against snake bites, and toothaches, and such. But, doesn't it feel like everyone is celebrating the snakes rather than warding them off?"

"I agree with you." Julia nods in the direction of the piazza. "Because the snakes are the main attraction."

"Yes, and all the charmers are so proud to have brought the beautiful snakes in, you can just see their admiration for the animals. It doesn't seem like they want them to be warded off or anything."

I think about my relationship with nature, I am scared of it, drawn to it, at times want to be lost in it, want to separate myself from it and its chaos. I am of course part of it. I am everything it is not.

"Maybe the snakes are for the goddess after all." Julia jokes. I am surprised she mentioned Angizia. I haven't mentioned my interest in her, or my completely unfounded theory at work.

"Angizia?" I manage to ask in my state of surprise. Now she is surprised I know who she's talking about.

"So in the ancient tradition, it is said that they would offer the snakes to her as part of the ceremony. Maybe after all these centuries, we are still making the offering."

I pull my knees into my chest, looking out at the landscape beyond the village, the road winding its way into the green hills and the snow-capped mountains beyond. I picture the snakes out there, slithering back to the wilderness, one wriggling, heaving mass of them again, going home to her.

We sip wine and crack open the stories of our lives until it's late. I am happy I chose to come, despite disappointing my family that I'd be gone another few days and the fact that I didn't make any clear connection, let alone get a semblance of understanding about the tradition. I stumble back to my room, a modest but comfortable nook on the upper floor of the apartment. The room is dark and cool, and I stumble to find the light switch for a moment, sliding my hand along the wall until it lands. I turn towards the bed and freeze. There, curled into a knotted spiral is the grandest snake I have seen all day, all my life. Her leather skin shines black and almost gold in the mellow orange light of the room. I am frozen in fear and awe, in shock and satisfaction. She's come back for me.

"She's come for the offering." I either whisper it softly or think it loudly. Either way, I know she's heard. "What does she want?"

The snake slowly uncoils herself and flicks her tongue just like the serpent in the fresco. She reveals her fangs.

"Name her something other than good," she hisses and rushes at me.

OF SIRENS
AND TWENTY-SOMETHINGS

The day was as August as it gets. Every smell was tinged with the sweet concoction of sunscreen, bug-spray, and sweat. Screen doors bounced shut throughout the neighborhood so frequently the sound became like a heartbeat, an almost frantic thumping testifying to our fear of wasting the last citrus rays of summer. I was used to the neurosis of my small coastal Massachusetts town, from how aggressively early the beach parking lot filled each morning by those committed to getting the "best sun" to the donning of shorts in mid-March as soon as the temperature hit upper-forties.

I was not immune to the anxiety, especially that summer, that first summer after graduating college, when going back to school didn't hang over those final weeks like a cranky cumulous cloud, nagging me that life couldn't all be about eating wild blackberries straight from the bushes off the bike path or reading on the hammock while the dog snores in the shade below or watching the world crystallize and drop into the ocean from an oar strewn across my lap, rocking in the harbor mid-kayak trip, mid-morning, mid the silent bobbing of sailboats. The summer was just as much the town's prime as it was my own, and even though I had graduated and hadn't gotten a yes from any of the 100 jobs I applied to yet, September still sat there like a slow, mean cat, swishing its tail, eyeing me and my joys.

Rolling onto my stomach, I saw my phone light up through the ratty yellow towel I had folded over to keep it from overheating in the noon sun. Clifton in 5. C is coming later but J and I are on her way! With the tides coming in, it made sense they wanted to go to the rocks. Soon the sliver of sand on the beach where I sunbathed would be gone. The crowd, which was already thinned out to a horizontal line against the seawall, would migrate to sit atop its rocky surface or on the grassy patches beside it. I checked my inbox again, then checked the sent box to make sure the follow-up email had really gone through. Zero and yes. Leaving Preston now. More like 15 for me.

When I got to the usual corner, just Katie was waiting there.

"Where's Jacqueline?" I shouted to her from across the street, hopping off my bike and locking it to the Conley's porch. My three-year stint as babysitter had the added privilege of a forever parking spot for my beloved grey Schwinn.

"She had to run home first and let out Bruno," Katie yelled back from the curb she always sat on, or at least since she discovered how that spot was in the direct line of vision from the third floor window of the Conley's house (a well-timed curtain ruffle was all it took to convince her), from where Dan Conley, if he was in town visiting his dad and stepmom, might enjoy the view of her stretching out her long tanned legs into the street and annoying passing cyclists. Even though she had the sexiest boyfriend of the group, Katie still craved male attention. I mean we all craved it, but she actually got a lot of it too.

She stood up and dusted off her butt, still yelling, "I guess her mom texted her and said the new medicine is making him shit like crazy, so she's gonna have to go back every couple hours."

A pair of approaching Lululemon moms with toddlered strollers glanced over at us, now standing together on the sidewalk.

"Cute."

"Yeah, well you know how her mom gets. She said to go down without her."

We started down the side street, a quiet, dreamy street that bloomed up in a short hill exactly half-way down. Flip-flops smacking our heels, we cut through the Jacobs' backyard, or I guess it was the Jacobs' before Mrs. Jacobs died and the rest of the family moved to the farthest point possible in our town's 4 square mile span. It was still the Jacobs' backyard. Regardless, no one seemed to mind that nearly every day we shaved down our walk by approximately 48 seconds by weaseling through their summersweet shrubs, fragrant at that time of year and frequented by white butterflies. I couldn't believe this was one of the last times Katie would be there with us, this summer different from the others because we were at the crossroads between school and "life after school," an expanse that unfurled itself towards eternity.

Finally, we reached the narrow dirt path, a splinter off the street nuzzled between a massive, nautical contemporary house and a tiny old cape cod cottage. Most people missed it the first time we invited them down there, trolling instead into the Lindens' driveway just a few feet away or discouraged by the sign halfway down the path that read Private Access for Clifton Rd. - Canal

St. Residents Only, Trespassers will be Prosecuted. Though the sign's authority was often dismantled by the frequent erasure of a certain "C," it still managed to keep a few of our more sheltered friends deterred.

In fact, the first time Jacqueline had taken me down to the rocks almost a decade before during the summer before 8th grade (it was the same day I learned how to comfortably insert a tampon for the first time, I remember bragging about it), she had barely convinced me to be such a rebel and to descend the rusty metal stairs. C'mon Han you're basically the Conley's other daughter, she had said. Besides no one gives a shit as long as we're not drinking or fucking. She'd end up doing both of those things at the rocks before we graduated high school. She always moved faster than me, and I wondered if that was why it felt like I was standing still. Nonetheless, her persuasion worked on me that first day in middle school as it had a million other times before then and would a million more.

I stooped down to smell the beach roses along the pebbled dirt, hearing Katie clang down the stairs ahead of me in that 1-2 way she always went down. Something about it reminded me of a toddler.

"You losers are so slow!" Jacqueline called out from the beginning of the path.

I stood up as she approached, we were both wearing the same beach cover-up we had each separately bought from Target in 10th grade and fought over for a week before discovering Kelly Reynolds also owned that exact cover-up, and it looked better on her than it ever would on either of us, so who cared. Sometimes this happened.

"How's shit?"

She passed me as she rolled her eyes, "Very funny. Don't even ask."

I followed behind her, looking down through the metal grates of the stairs at the wiry gabions filled with multicolored stones which made up the enormous defense from the surf. The wire-mesh crates were themselves arranged like a staircase for ogres or giants who might emerge from the medieval-looking, cliff-lined shore. Certain steps always smelt like dried seaweed and fish. Others more crisp and less salty, like a fresh sun if you could bottle it. By the bottom, the whole combination settled and combined into one perfectly ocean-y fume.

I stepped down to the flat, granite floor pocketed with tide-pools and already half submerged. On a lazier, cooler day we would have parked it there. Katie was already moving over the mid-sized boulders to the left. She was tall enough, her legs could span some of the larger gaps between them, though lanky enough no one would ever say she made that look elegant. Beyond her the cliff rose up, our ledge about six feet from the water's surface, vacant, and calling. Off to the right, the raft-like dock we swam out to on that very first day was occupied by a mother and son, about eight years old if I were to guess. Even far enough away that they looked like miniatures, I could see she was sprawled out, starfish style on the dock, while he endlessly tossed himself into the blue, his limbs flailing out in a different formation each time. In all my years coming down to the rocks, I had never displayed such a lack of caution. The first time I had stood immobilized on the final wooden stair, my knees already submerged, holding the sea-soaked rope and thinking I'll never make it to the dock.

I started my slow maneuver over the boulders, plopping down on my butt or monkeying on hands and feet in the spots I always did.

"Hannah, any word on the MassArt job?" Katie shouted.

"Not yet!" I called back, teetering on a wobbly rock, on wiggly flip-flops.

"Assholes." Jacqueline said from a few rocks ahead of me.

I shrugged, almost losing my balance. My friends' disappointment was starting to compound on my mom's. Not to mention, my own, holding out for a lowly administrative job with the pathetic hopes of taking lunch breaks with Jacqueline who would start her research assistantship at Beth Israel in a couple weeks and moving into the city after the months it would take to save enough money to do so. Jaqueline already had an apartment lined up for September.

"I'm sure they're just super busy with the semester about to start," Katie offered, waiting for us to finish our trek. I appreciated her positivity, would miss it balancing out our somewhat cynical group of friends when she went off to med school across the country the following week. We clanked over the pebbly part of the beach, listening to the snoring waves topple stones like the ones beneath our feet. That all four of us had managed to eke out one more summer here seemed both impossible and inevitable.

In order to reach the side of the cliff with the familiar divots and ridges, we had to walk a few feet out into the water. We slung our towels around our shoulders and took off our shoes. The cold was shocking even this late in the summer, even just up to our ankles. The two of them hoisted themselves up in three quick movements.

Jacqueline turned to give me a hand from the nearest "step" to the top, knowing full well that if I lifted myself the way I always did I'd scrape my left knee in the place I always did, on the annoying patch of rough rock I'd been cussing out for years. I'd always been too scared to try a different maneuver, accepting a perpetually scabbed knee in exchange for any doubt as to whether I'd make it. It had taken a long running campaign to get me up the rock in the first place, a campaign fueled by a July sighting of the seniors (they had long graduated high school at that time but would always be 'the seniors' as they had been when we were freshmen) sipping coronas and looking quite kingly themselves, on that lofty, stone throne. It's crazy how seniors can look so adult when you're a freshman, and then look so babyish when you're in college. It's like our minds are always avoiding the growing up part, nudging it further and further into the future. I wonder if I'll be a forty-year old, idolizing the 50-year-olds for being real grown-ups.

We laid out our towels on the flattest areas and littered our cover-ups. I propped myself up on my left side, crooking my left hip into the familiar scoop. Katie sat on the edge and bounced her heels against the rock, on her left ankle she had a stack of string anklets. Jacqueline pulled pistachios out of her bag, popping them whole into her mouth to suck the salt off, cracking them with her teeth, and pulling the shells out of her mouth to add to the neat pile she made. A small mountain had accumulated before Katie caved, "Guys I don't think I can wait for Celine."

Sweat had started to roll from my temple down my neck. "Yeah me neither."

"Did she say when she'd be back from Tom's?" Katie asked.

"It's Celine. Would it make a difference if she gave us an ETA?" Jacqueline held out the bag of pistachios to me before putting them away. I noticed her blue nails were chipped in a perfect every-other pattern.

"Oh she was at Tom's again?" I felt a pang at being the only one who didn't know this. Also, if Celine paired up, I'd be the only single one left of the group, having dumped my college boyfriend Eddie at the start of our last semester because I didn't want him to sway my glamorous post-grad plans and his apartment always smelt like deli meat and dirty towels. Not to mention, he only liked to talk about school friends and school teams, and I worried that when we graduated we'd immediately turn into one of those couples who sits across from one another at a restaurant and doesn't talk but just chews at each other slowly and intently. Eddie had been my first real boyfriend, and no one, least of all me, expected it to last more than a few months. Before Eddie my friends stopped telling me about their love lives because they felt badly I hadn't experienced it yet. Maybe Celine didn't tell me she was going over Tom's because she pitied me, single again, no juicy gossip to share. Sometimes it felt like boys were the only thing my friends found interesting enough to talk about.

"Third night in a row she's driven all the way up to Portsmouth. I'd say she likes him." Jacqueline smirked, standing up so we knew she didn't want to wait either.

The sun, directly overhead and relentless, was bordering on torturous. I rolled onto my stomach feeling the heat from the rock beneath my towel, before waggling to my knees and standing up. I knew the motion was geriatric, with my hands on my thighs to keep steady. The sun had sapped my energy, leaving me dizzy and weak. We walked to the edge. The hot granite scorched our feet. We looked out over the dimpled, light-dappled sea.

***

"Hannah Elise Miller! Stop thinking so goddamn much and get in!" Jacqueline called out to me. She had been buoying just a few yards away from me for what felt like a century, having practiced treading water with no arms at summer camp the year before. My feet had gone numb in the June water, and I could see her lips start to purple. "I'll meet you at the dock!" I said, feeling the pressure and adding her impending pneumonia to my list of concerns including barnacles, sharks, and knocking my head against the rock, concussing and drowning. I had learned to catastrophize before I even turned 13. The dock sat just yards away, a goal, an island. "Like hell you will!" She shouted between shivers, paddling over to the wooden planks someone had drilled into the rocks to create the stairs, the last of which my feet had cemented into. I knew she was going to pull me in.

***

"Okay, 1, 2, 3!" Katie called out for us. We jumped together. After the initial shocks and shrieks there was always a quick silence. We were out of the ocean and then, suddenly, we were in it, we were a part of it. Freezing but weightless. Invigorated.

***

Before she was close enough to pull me in, I stepped off the final stair, plugging my nose and sending a wave into her face. I saw her eyes pulse wider in surprise before going under. Without the forward momentum of a leap, the rock loomed below me and I felt my feet graze something mossy and slick just as my sinking slowed to a near halt. I shot up, knifing the surface, unable to wipe all the panic off my expression. We exploded into laughter. What had I been scared of? What was I always so scared of? I felt the tampon balloon inside of me and buoy down. I did my best to maneuver it under the water's surface, doggy paddling behind her on our way to the dock, still giggling off my jitters and praying that this was supposed to happen in water.

***

Within moments of leaping off our ledge my body was used to the water temperature, wishing the iciness would last just a smidge longer. Every so often one of us would dive under and glide out towards the horizon, quickly turning back and rejoining the conversation. I loved how at that time of year, at that time of day, the light streamed in emerald from below the water's surface.

"When do you think we'll get to meet him?" Katie asked, floating on her back.

"Who?"

"Tom! Keep up, Hannah!"

"Oh, right. Maybe she'll bring him to Labor Day?"

"Are we still doing the cookout at Crocker?" Jacqueline asked, treading slowly.

"I assumed so. Katie will you still be here?"

Katie's eyes were closed, "Nope, moving in that weekend."

"Don't leave!" I yelled out and splashed her in the face. She spit the salty water out.

Soon we were all treading in a small circle. "Don't bring it up! Besides, I'll be back for Thanksgiving. It's not any different than any other year."

Jacqueline pouted, "Boooo. Well you better come home before then. Besides, Celine will probably have a new Tom by then!" And I'll probably be right here, still.

Katie laughed, "New Tom, Portsmouth Tom, or no Tom. Thanksgiving's the first break I have that's long enough."

We all started to float off again before Katie spoke, "You know it seems kind of exciting?"

We turned to look at her so she could explain her train of thought, "Like introducing someone new to the group. The whole dating thing. You know, that was always fun."

"What do you mean?" Jaqueline asked.

"Like us talking about what you think of him, and hearing what he thinks of all of you guys. All the hype."

Jacqueline and I looked at each other, not really following. I did my best to understand, "You know we all love Matt, right?"

Now Katie seemed a bit annoyed that we weren't listening intently enough. "No, I know you guys love Matt, and Matt loves you all, and I love Matt, and he loves me. But like sometimes I get jealous of Celine and the newness of it all. The excitement. Does that make sense?"

I made a joke about being single like I always did when it came to the subject. Could she really be jealous of a new relationship when she at least had one of her own? Did she even realize who she was talking to? Matt was moving with her across the country, she'd be a doctor with 3 kids before I ever even purchased a couch instead of plucking some decrepit thing off the street and praying there were no bugs in it.

Jacqueline nodded, "Yeah I guess it's weird I won't ever do that again."

Now Katie and I looked at each other in confusion. Jaqueline started to make her way to the pebbly beach, the shore sloping to her disadvantage and the tide pulling her back like a lover who wants just five more minutes.

"Now what are you saying?" I asked, trying to hide my insecurity with a laugh. Jaqueline had only been with Justin a year, it felt like we had just met him. Thinking back to the moment I had met Justin at last year's Friendsgiving, I remembered feeling inspired from that event to break up with Eddie. They had seemed so much more compatible, whispering little jokes to each other throughout the meal, bringing a pie they had made together, exchanging little pecks when they thought no one was looking or maybe when they knew someone was. Maybe it had been a mistake not to give Eddie more of a shot. Sure, I felt a slight annoyance whenever he texted me, and the sex had gone from below mediocre to above mediocre back down to mediocre. But he had always taken me to dinner and ordered an appetizer. Not to mention he always asked how my day was and seemed to listen before asking what I ate during the day. Now here I was at 22, single and jobless, while the others kept moving.

Jacqueline turned over her shoulder, pausing belly deep in the water, fixing the string from the top of her bikini which had slung all the way around her left shoulder. She looked golden, with the sun almost directly behind her head illuminating the little auburn frizzies coming off her bun which was already starting to dry. What did she mean by that? "I mean I know I'm gonna marry Justin," she said proudly, calmly.

Everything was already set for everyone else. What was with the rush to be adults? Wasn't this so much better? Why would anyone want to leave? The seaweed nodded all around us.

***

When I reached the dock, Jacqueline stood there balancing, arms and legs spread out like a weird sort of surfer. She didn't have boobs yet either, but something in her slenderness seemed so sure of herself, so adult. Her teeth chattered from the wind on her frigid skin. "Hans, I think this is gonna be our spot. Look at the shore from here." She rubbed her upper arms to warm up. I used the wobbly ladder to pull myself onto the strangely carpeted plank. The rocking was majestic and calming; I steadied myself using the ladder's railing and looked back at the shore we had swam from. The waves crashed white into the black rock face, and I was high off the accomplishment of daring that dark, whirling, mad water. I was so grateful I had a friend who would show me such adventure, who would take me with her. Jacqueline put her arm around my shoulder and we waved frantically at the houses along the coast. Blood dribbled down my legs.

***

"Celine!"

I followed Jacqueline's gaze to the metal stairs, where Celine clomped down, one hand on the railing, one hand waving back to Jacqueline, who had made it to dry land before Katie and I were ready to get out. Celine scanned the beach and saw where we swam. "Hey lady!" I called out. "There's our lover girl!" Katie yelled. "Sorry we couldn't wait!"

"I don't blame you!" She yelled back from the bottom stair. She hadn't even made it to the nest of boulders before she started removing clothing. "It's brutal out here."

When she got to the pebbles she chatted with Jacqueline for a minute before wading in, skipping the whole climb and leap. Jacqueline took her things and brought them up to our ledge, lying out in the sun while the three of us swam.

The afternoon went like it always did, in and out, freezing and sweltering, the sun lowering, the light thickening into a delicious pink-orange. Jacqueline went home to let the dog out, and when she returned Katie had gone to meet Matt for a movie. Celine left soon after to remind her parents she was still alive. Now the warm rock felt heavenly and comforting beneath my towel, and I thought about dozing off and dozed off. We didn't talk for a while. Eventually Jacqueline turned over from the side she was curled up on, reading her book. "What do you say, Han, one more dunk?" The tide was too low by now to jump. We shimmied down the side we had climbed, dumped our bags among the pebbles, and waded out into the water. It never felt as cold the second, third, eighth time we went in each day. But then, somehow, our bodies would reset overnight and brace for the inevitable constriction after the first submersion of the next day. Impossible and inevitable. By the time we waded out to a point deep enough to dunk, the sun was nosing the horizon and our faces were glowing embers over a purple-green sea. We squinted, sighing how gorgeous, how lucky, each of us bobbing along in what, it occurred to me then, had never been the same ocean.

PORTRAIT OF A LADY AS POMONA

"Be silent echoing rumour:
believe the god who speaks about himself."

Propertius, Book IV.2, Translated A.S. Kline

We met in my gardens, though that first time, I admit, I did not know. I was accustomed to visitors, as creator of the most renowned orchard in the land, my beauty just as famous. While my sisters preferred the wilderness, the woods and rivers, I always had a fondness for the nature I could control. They frolicked, I nourished. The trees nourished me back. Though I lived in my Eden and wanted nothing, I constantly feared. Dancing satyrs and Pans haunted my gates, threatened to steal me, to take me for theirs. Old Silvanus pursued me, and Priapus with his enormous (though rumor has it, faulty) weapon. I did not admit suitors, I turned away all men who asked for me. But you arrived, in your first disguise, with a pruning knife quite like mine. You even had the small cuts on your hands and forearms of someone who is used to taming thorny vines and splintered branches. Dirt under your fingernails. I let you in, unlike the rest, you who wanted to learn from the best gardener in all of Rome. You watched me in the orchard. I felt your eyes on me while I watered the roots just beginning to thirst and cut back the overgrown branches. I heard the extra wetness in your mouth when you complimented my work, sent you away with a basket of plums.

***

Liam and I had been married two months before the question arose, "So when are you having kids?"

The first time it happened was at a work function. Marci, our middle-aged administrative receptionist who everyone agreed could never EVER retire, asked me over a platter of sad mini quiches. Both her and the waitress looked at me wide-eyed. I was naïve then, stupid.

"Oh, we actually aren't having children."

Marci made a sound like coughing or choking or gasping or maybe no sound at all, but enough movement to send the waitress away.

"Ever?"

Foolish me! I was shocked that someone I barely knew could pass judgement so openly and unabashedly!

I laughed, "Um, well, we aren't planning to."

This seemed to comfort her, which made me even more uncomfortable, "Oh well two of mine weren't planned either," she chuckled.

***

I should have known it was you the next time, the smell of fresh mown grass on your skin. You had a new face. You wore a wreath made of hay above a tanned forehead. You wore broad shoulders, beads of sweat, and an unrefined tongue. I accepted your baskets of barley and wheat, newly sliced by the scythe you carried over your back. I plucked grapes while you told me of your harvests, noticed your eyes drop to my upper lip, my wrists. But when I offered them to you, you refused, you said this is not a trade but a gift. Hunger drenched your words, and you were gone.

I was expecting you when you came on your third visit. Again a new face, a new prop. Weeks went by, you came to me: a soldier, a sailor, fisherman, shepherd, butcher, wanderer, gardener. You watched, drooled, worshipped. Your visits became more frequent. I feigned ignorance, hoping that as long as you thought you fooled me, I held some power over you. In reality I did not know what to do. I knew your desire grew, that soon you would reveal yourself to me. Immobilized by indecision, I weighed my options. If I turned you away, you Vertumnus, god of seasons, god of change, how would you punish me? Would I face an endless winter? Or worse? I could reveal my hand, say, *Vertumnus, I know it is you. You embody a new form everyday now, visiting my orchards, drooling over my fruits. When you arrive my pear blossoms bloom, my grapes ripen, fill with juice, and weigh down their vine. You cannot contain yourself. You think you fool me with your scythes and goads and ladders, but the heart of a man is never hidden for long. Put down your props and reveal yourself.* But if I did that, the end would rush in. You'd have me or you'd end me, or take away the one place I had any power in this world, the only joy I took in my existence. I would be forced into an eternal motherhood, the confines of being a good goddess-mother were a prison compared to the confines of my orchard.

My insides coil to think about that time. The paralysis. You every day, filling my entire sacred orchard with your desire, and the terrible dancing of the satyrs every night. The woods crept up to my gates, threatening to overtake me and my gardens with their wildness. And if I ran away, and took to those very woods, I knew I would be swallowed whole. In the hours without you, I threw myself into my labor, my hands into the soil. Every fruit tree hummed with happiness, the orchard blooming in a Pythagorean perfection. So while it pains me to think of those last days in limbo, I am simultaneously filled with the most acute longing. Longing for that fullness of being alone, of existing within the product of my own genius. A time when I could create with my hands, when I was something more than everyone's mother.

***

Marci was the tip of the iceberg. For the next few years, every time the question arose I would be met terror after terror from co-workers, friends, relatives, friends of relatives, co-workers of friends, relatives of co-workers: *Won't you feel left out when all your friends have kids? What are you going to do with all that extra time? Didn't you ever want to be a Mom? I'm sure you'll change your mind eventually. I said the same thing, but can't imagine what purpose my life would have without my kids. You know, don't wait too long, the older you get the more chances for complications and mental illness. Does Liam know this? Aren't your parents disappointed?*

***

So yes, love, I chose you. But I am not what you think I am. When you came to me that day, it's true, I did not recognize you this time. You had never appeared to me as a woman before, and neither had you chosen a body so old. It didn't occur to me then, that the day you would finally choose to show your face, you would try something new. So I saw you, hunched over at my gate, admiring my land. You looked tired, worn from a long walk, a longer life. Your parched lips screamed for water, your thin, wobbling legs for rest. It was your best guise yet. In that moment, I yearned for any companion that wasn't you, that wasn't hunting me, threatening to pluck me like one of my fruits and keep me for themselves. And to see an old woman there, who would ask nothing of me except a drink from my fountain and a rest under my trees, who may have a nugget of wisdom from her years to help free me from my imprisonment. That was the only day you knew something of my heart.

You couldn't speak until after a drink, so rasped were you with thirst. We sat beneath the apple tree, and I let you lean some of your weight on my shoulder. At last you spoke.

"I have never seen an orchard like this in all my life." Your voice was crackly, coming to life. I thanked you, and you looked deep into my eyes. All the blood went rotten in my veins. Fear thundered in my eardrums; my mouth filled with a metallic taste. "Though they are by no means as lovely as you, dear," I heard *you* say, as you planted a warm, wet kiss on the corner of my mouth. You, who couldn't contain yourself anymore, who thought I would accept this woman's affections as protective, maternal even. How dumb you thought me, you still think me.

Everything in me went ice, and you began your long-planned coup, mistaking my shock for rapt attention. But I had already chosen my path, so throughout your great monologue, I tried to play my part. I painted myself captivated as you explained to me the symbiotic relationships around me. How the grapevine, encircling and adorning the elm tree, no longer rests on the ground. The tree is made more beautiful and more frequented by visitors, who have little use for its leaves alone. Those very systems that I built and created, you taught me about and used to capture me.

"See everything must be married, union makes life more beautiful, more fruitful," you cooed, at last arriving to your point.

I couldn't bring myself to speak, to agree with you. You who sat there denying any worth I had in the world without you.

"Listen to my words, dear. I love you more than you can know. How long have you turned away marriage? How many gods have come to your gates? You are a stubborn soul, but it's time for you to accept love. Be wise. Vertumnus loves you as no other ever has and no other ever will. Marry him, and he will take any form that you desire. He will fill your orchards with apples. Marry him, Pomona. The gods demand it!"

***

Liam, to be fair, was much better about dealing with the question. He'd laugh it off in that way men can where they don't say anything at all, but people accept that as an answer. I couldn't let it go. I wanted to print a pamphlet, call it "Why I'm Not Having Kids and Why You Don't Have to Either!" I'd include financial projections, photos of Liam and me in exotic locations, authorized signatures from my parents, schedule templates that included activities like "read a book" or "yoga retreat" without any "soccer drop-offs" or "breastfeeding." I couldn't handle the disappointment anymore. I was used to "how exciting!" and "good for you!" whenever I shared my next steps: going to a good college, choosing a good major, getting a good job, marrying a good man. And yet, without motherhood, I would never be a good girl again.

***

You were crazed now, filled with the sort of desire you know you are finally close to satisfying. I opened my mouth, commanding myself to say yes, to play the part I had practiced. But in the second of hesitation, you grabbed my hands. My slightest flinch revealed a disgust which you thought was still lack of convincing.

"Are you not god fearing? Do you not know what happens to women who turn away love? Have you not heard the story of Anaxarete?" Your warped nails dug into my palms. "Cold, stone-hearted Anaxarete, who turned away poor Iphis so many times, so cruelly, he gave up hope," your eyes swelled and glistened with emotion. "Poor Iphis who hung himself from the crossbeam over her door, so that his feet thudding against the door sounded like a knock." I shuddered, if logic wasn't working, fear was what it would take?

"Pomona, do you know what happened to Anaxarete? Do you know what it does to a person, to see the funeral procession, the mother and father grey with grief, knowing your cruelty created this unnecessary tragedy?"

This was it, this was your final push. I shook my head.

"The stone in her heart spread to her entire body."

In that moment you were more honest with me than ever before. *You are trapped*, is what you really said. You can live like stone in a dying garden for the rest of eternity. It does not matter that you are the goddess of fruit trees, I am the god of the seasons, you exist within me and because of me. You can be mine, my good wife, you can bear child after child, goddess of fruit, it's your destiny.

If only I had screamed, "Let me be stone!" But I was not and am not as strong as Anaxarete, who at least became what was inside her all along.

At last you revealed yourself, young, strong, Vertumnus, bursting out like sun from a dreary cloud, "Pomona," you said, in the wet, hungry voice I had always known, "submit, marry me, I beg you, and live a life with neither frost nor storm."

I never had a choice. I accepted you.

***

Eventually I learned how to deflect the questions and judgement, which most often meant lying. "Maybe someday. Who knows. When we're ready." And then an odd moment came when people stopped asking us. They forgot we didn't have any or assumed we were too old to be trying or thought maybe there was a sensitive reason we didn't have them. I had nearly forgotten the guilty tumult of that period until a few weeks ago when I was visiting my sister's family. Sitting outside with my seven-year-old niece, while she waggled a hula hoop around her hips, dropping it every few seconds, I cheered her on.

"Auntie Meg," she said in a moment of repose between attempts. "Why don't I have any cousins?"

In that moment the guilt came flooding back. "Well, because me and Uncle Liam don't have any kids."

She stood there in go-position holding the hoop at her waist for a second looking at me, "But why not?"

I didn't want to get into the complexities here. "Your Uncle Liam and I, we, well, we decided we didn't want to a long, long time ago."

She swung the hoop and started swaying. The hoop made it twice around before falling. Picking it up again—I had to commend her for her perseverance—she asked without even looking up, "So you're nobody's mom?"

It sounded like, "So you're nobody?"

***

I don't go to my orchard anymore, though I hear you keep the apples in harvest all year. The place is no longer mine, but instead it's your plaything, like my body. What is one bloom when you can turn a whole harvest, shuffle a season? I lost all faith in the power of my labor. Everything is mutable. You stopped coming to me too, surprising me with new forms and guises. Because you know what you have done. You told me a story of a man who killed himself for love, and a woman who turned to stone. You told me this so I would marry you. You who watched but never understood me, you who trapped me between two options for my demise: be yours or be nothing at all. I chose wrong. Still, you are left with a stone woman. You tried to be good to me, but you had already sapped my power, my joy, my life. All those years of finding purpose in my labor, of nurturing and taming and sweating to create my own place in this world, all an illusion, when it's up to the gods what labor I am destined for. I am not asking for your tears, my Vertumnus. You are nostalgic for someone who never existed. Do not cry for your lullaby story, whoever, whatever you are beneath the swirling, shifting surface. I will let you keep your story, the story of the yummy apple nymph you tricked into love, into becoming the benevolent mother-goddess within her all along. Oh how people will love us and our blooming, abundant, happy marriage. Do what you will with it: rouse the winds, summon the storms, turn the earth on its axis to let that story be known. But not without first hearing mine.

HERA'S SPRING

Her oldest son drove her to the airport in the wee hours of the morning. He was 24, not quite living at home but not quite living on his own either. He had an apartment in the city, but still came for dinner more often than normal. She struggled not to do his laundry, because she knew he should, but she also knew he would let it go too long between washes. It wasn't a failure to launch situation, more like an extended launch, like that moment when they untie a boat from the dock and without the stability of a taut rope it bobs down in the waves before finding its own rocking balance. He had a fine job and an acceptable, if nerdy, social life. But neither of them could untie just yet. She told herself it's because he's the oldest, with his younger sister in college. When she'd come home for breaks, they both would tuck themselves back into the nest, the three of them would cook lavish dinners or assemble junk food meals and watch TV until their eyes hurt. But how could she be sure this wasn't just another case of her burying her head in the sand, the way she did with her husband? Wasn't the media always warning about quiet, nerdy white boys? But while with her husband there had been those flags of distance, coldness, jitteriness, and even vanity—only observed retrospectively of course, her son had always been warm, unassuming, quietly sweet. He had woken up at 4 a.m. to get her there on time that day without complaining, without prying too much about her last minute decision to run off to Greece after years of pushing off international travel for a more "convenient" time. Surely all roads couldn't lead to predator, right?

She had actually gotten closer to her kids since the divorce, though that makes sense given the circumstances—they dutifully stood by the side of the wronged—it surprised her given she'd been such a mess the last year. For months her world had become like a formless blob. Nothing made sense anymore, nothing was clear: how they'd tell the kids, where she would live permanently, what they'd do about money, about health insurance, all the ways they'd untangle their lives from each other. But even when the details were figured out, her life had still felt amorphous. Who had she been for these 53 years of her life, and for what? The future was too overwhelming to consider all at once. Unmoored and barely afloat, she had tried to take each day one by one, the past and the future two different beasts she avoided at all costs. At the end of the transition there was the sad truth that her day to day routine hadn't changed that much, and most days it was easier to pretend he had been hit by a truck.

"You sure you want to go all that way alone?" he asked, as they pulled up to the terminal. "I mean, it's not too late to rebook when I can get some time off and–"

"Honey," she laughed. "It's my job to worry. And besides, I won't be alone–the tour group, remember?"

"I know, I know. But, like, a bus full of strange high school Latin teachers who you have absolutely nothing in common with isn't all that different from being alone." She couldn't blame him for his confusion. Trying to write off the specific history-buff tour as the more acceptable eat-pray-love moment for someone her age wasn't exactly an easy feat. But it's not like she could tell him the real reason she chose to go on this one.

"It's only a week, sweetie. And who knows? Maybe I'll have more in common with those weirdo Latin nerds than you think!"

"Sure," he chuckled. "Well, have fun. And text me when you land please."

She agreed and zipped up her anxieties to put on a brave face. "I'll try not to go too wild." It was the first time she's ever travelled alone, and she had chosen the tour because it was affordable (her settlement more than covered it), brief (it lined up with many schools' spring break so was crammed into one week), and because it would take her to the fountain, one of only three tours she found that would do so. The café she managed would survive her absence, she assured herself as she went through the line to check her bag, her kids would be fine for a week, she repeated like a mantra in her head as she went through security, she'd be back soon, she told herself as she boarded.

As soon as the plane took off, something in her shifted, she was actually going to Greece. *What am I doing?* She thought, at the same time she thought, *I am such a cliché.* She busied herself with distractions, took out the itinerary packet that had arrived a couple of weeks ago, the words "The Hidden Peloponnese" sprawled across the front cover in a corny font, and started thumbing through the activities she had skimmed over. There was only one site on the itinerary that mattered to her: Agia Moni. She would have to wait until the 5th day to see it, but in the meantime, she'd traverse a country she had never even stepped foot in, hike up to the acropolis of

Corinth and down to the caves of Diros, have lunch in the ancient Spartan city of Mystras, pick olives by hand, and sip wine from the famous Domaine Bairaktaris. She wondered who would be joining her on the trek, but then decided it didn't really matter. For once, she didn't want to focus on whether she fit in or whether people liked her, she just wanted to be far from home and on the path to renewal.

***

They gathered in the hotel just an hour after she arrived and made quick introductions before boarding everyone on the coach bus. It was the first of many times the middle-aged (generous) group would be rushed along. There were 15 of them. She was the only one on the tour who wasn't in the education field, which wasn't surprising given the title and itinerary of the trip. History nerds never leave school, she thought, with more admiration than arrogance. She had always been on the cusp of being great at school, and decades ago she had loved history too, though math had always won her over. She liked predictability, and history had always sat a touch too on the chaotic end of the spectrum for her.

"Now, where are you coming from?" The woman who had moments ago introduced herself as "Patricia, but you can call me Patty" asked her after taking the seat next to her on the bus. They were part of the smaller "singles" contingent, as most other members had travelled with a spouse or buddy– so it made sense Patty wanted to befriend her.

"New York," She answered, thinking how despite

herself she was relieved someone sat next to her. "Upstate. And yourself?"

"Oh wow!" Patty exclaimed though there was nothing amazing about being from upstate New York. "I'm from Virginia, but I guarantee we were on the same flight over from Newark!"

Patty explained that she taught Latin at the local university, though was trying to design a Greek mythology course. Just as she was about to take a turn explaining what brought her on the trip, they were interrupted by their excursion guide. She was relieved.

"Welcome aboard!" The young Greek woman, who couldn't be older than 25, began. "In case you missed it, I am Sophia and I can't wait to get to know you over the next week. I hope you all had a relaxing flight here to Athens today. I know you are probably tired, but we find the best way to deal with jet lag is to waste no time at all, have a full day, and then you will surely sleep well tonight!" The bus laughed though it wasn't really a joke. The guide laid out their insane day—the only one they'd spend in the city—as they started the short drive to the Acropolis. As Sophia went on, she noticed Patty take out her camera and start to take blurry pictures every 30 seconds, the fat glare of the bus window streaking through each one. Finally, Sophia sat for the last five minutes of the ride. Patty paused taking pictures and turned to her.

"Now you never told me what it is you do."

"Oh," she laughed awkwardly. "I run a restaurant, a café."

"Oh, how fantastic!" Patty exclaimed, though there is nothing fantastic about managing a café.

"Thank you," she sort-of accepted the sort-of-compliment anyway. "It's no big deal."

"I'm sure it's lovely."

She took her phone out to show Patty a recent picture of the quaint café, with its flowerboxes, twinkly-lit courtyard, and chalk board signs. *It is quite lovely*, she admitted to herself.

Patty took the phone and zoomed in, explaining she didn't have her glasses handy (maybe that explains the terrible, blurry photography). Though when she tried to zoom, she accidentally swiped to the picture before it, one of her two kids sipping hot cocoa in the courtyard.

"Oh ooopsie," Patty laughed, going back to the empty café picture. "What a beautiful place."

"Thank you."

"Really, looks so charming. And, are those your children?"

"They are. Laura and Andrew, 20 and 24. Do you have any?"

"Well they look like great kids, just beautiful. I do, one boy, 33. Welcomed my first grandchild last year, another boy."

Patty took out the obligatory baby picture. She was old school and kept a printed one in her pocketbook. "Swear that baby looks more like my husband than my son did, isn't it crazy how it can work out like that?" She wondered at the casual mention of a husband, why Patty hadn't decided to bring hers along for the tour, but decided she didn't want to open up any can of worms by asking.

She nodded and completed the obligatory oohs and aahs, before they pulled into the parking lot. As she gathered her backpack and water bottle, she looked at her phone again before putting it away, the picture of her kids still open. There had been no skipping a generation when it came to her son, he was the spitting image of his father, the man she had been married to for nearly 30 years before he cheated on her: lanky, mystical hazel eyes that shift from honey to sage to almond, and that square chin with the slightest hint of a dimple. The chin that she could recognize anywhere, the chin she had recognized last year, the chin that sent her whole world into a spiral.

It was that chin she had seen on his Tinder account. An account which her technologically unsavvy husband had been sneaky enough to download to his computer, but too stupid to clear his history after every use. She didn't normally use his computer, but she had left hers in the café and needed to book plane tickets. She never understood why she opened his history though. She didn't even think about it, she just did it. It was like something possessed her, half her mind was thinking about the plane tickets, the other half was thinking about her Lean Cuisine with 48 seconds left in the microwave, and yet here she was in his browser history. Maybe part of her knew. But even when she saw the web address, fourth from the top, she was in denial. Must be a work thing. Maybe there is a different Tinder website for computers. Maybe he lent someone his computer? But there his stupid chin was when she opened the tab. A fake name, slightly altered age, only pictures from the moustache down, and a bio that read "Questions? More pics? Just knock." She would've recognized that chin a mile away, but it wasn't her he was worried about. He had known she would never be on there. She had felt acid bubble at the back of her throat, her whole face went hot.

Surely this couldn't have worked? The microwave had been going off for minutes now, as she poked around the site until she found the messages. There were dozens of them, stretching back over a year, from girls half their age to women she could have seen in her empty-nester yoga class. She read through all of them half-blurred with angry steaming tears, counted the ones he had actually met, responded to a couple with fiery warnings about the man they thought they were talking to. Their world was over. The beautiful man she had spent nearly thirty years with, who had been her entire sexual experience of the world, the father to her children and her longest held friend, was now as disgusting to her as the cold, congealing meal rotting in the microwave.

She put her phone in her bag and stepped out to see the most famous Greek temple of all time looming above. It was a structure that emanates miracles, having lasted thousands of years presiding over the ancient city. There was nothing "hidden" about it, but no tour of Greece would be complete without a visit. It was mammoth and commanding, despite its ruin. *Sometimes the most supernatural thing to do, is to stand,* she thought. She had arrived.

***

By the third day, Patty was her best friend, confidante, and perpetual bus buddy. She was maternal and consistently positive, which had been irritating at first, but by then felt familiar and safe. Patty explained the myths and references she wasn't familiar with in a way that was patient without being patronizing, detailed but not exhausting (unlike some of the other tour group members). In the 2 evenings they'd been there, when most everyone went straight to their rooms to pass out, the two of them had taken a nightcap at the hotel bar, swapping stories about their families, Patty's trials and triumphs in academia, the divorce. Patty had been married for over 30 years and understood the exhaustion of it all. Their friendship was, they both knew it, temporary, but intense in the way bonds can be when miles from home and surrounded by newness.

So when they arrived at the winery in the late afternoon, a relaxing break from the site tours and information overloads, the two of them sat side by side. The property, located in the ancient valley of Nemea, was modest and surrounded on all sides by neat green vines. After the customary cellar tour and spiel, they began pouring. They started with a sweet white, followed by a dry rosé she could have easily downed a bottle of, then a Cabernet Sauvignon from Corinth. They finished with a bold red that had a surprising spice and asked everyone which they would like a full glass of. Her and Patty looked at each other in approval, before singing in unison, "the rosé!" She was tipsy but realized the rest of the group was too. It had been hours since lunch, and the pours were monstrously generous. She felt like giggling for the first time in months, really full on giggling and skipping through the vines. They put out plates of cheese and olives, which were gone instantly, before letting them know they had an hour to relax, walk the gorgeous grounds, shop, or drink. The light was so beautiful coming through the hills, she wanted to cry. She took a picture and sent it to her kids, with the wine glass in view.

They'd make fun of her for being "basic," but she'd enjoy every second of that.

"For the kids?" Patty asked her, and she realized it was just the two of them at the picnic table.

"They're so going to make fun of me for this." She put her phone away, and raised her glass to Patty, "To fun!"

"To fun!" Patty clinked with her, and laughed her boisterous mom laugh.

"I can't remember the last time I had so much fun."

"There's really nothing like travel, is there?"

"There isn't. Nothing like travel...and wine! I might add!" She polished off the last of her glass and plopped it down.

"You got that right."

They sat admiring the landscape for a minute before Patty piped up again, "And what about that sommelier? Did you see him? Phew! I could've used a glass of him!" She honked, flushed and happy.

It occurred to her that she hadn't even noticed the sommelier, if he was handsome or not, she still hadn't fine-tuned her brain to the fact that she was single. Her brain hadn't fully registered the thought. "Was he cute?"

"Cute?! Puppies are cute. He was divine. Go in and get a bottle, just to see him! Seriously, he reminds me of this old flame of mine from my college days. You really didn't notice him?"

"Patty!"

They hooted into the hills while Patty reminisced over her youthful conquests.

"I have only been with one man." The words slipped out of her mouth before she decided to say them.

Patty looked at her surprised, "The asshole?"

She nodded. They had lost their virginities to each other when they were seventeen. She had only even kissed two boys before him. In a bed that was neither of theirs, they fumbled and laughed through the awkwardness. It wasn't great or even close to good for either of them, but it was a memory they returned to often with fondness. They had figured it out together, learned together. In college they experimented in all the typical ways and a couple strange ones. They scoured each other's minds for every possible inkling of a fantasy before settling into a routine that got them both off in an acceptable amount of time. So later on, when her friends gave her crap for having only slept with one person, she didn't care. She liked that she could associate her entire sexual narrative with him. She felt completely known. He had been entirely hers. They lived in a world that they had built together, and that was theirs alone.

Now it was different, and she knew that the story had always been a sham. She was almost drunk enough to tell a jovial Patty the real reason she wanted to go to Agia Moni so badly, but she didn't. She couldn't admit it to herself really. They, like gibbering teens, plotted how to give the sommelier her number, and she felt the weight of her confession lift. In less than two days she would be at the fountain, but it started to feel like the entire trip was a part of her transformation.

***

At last, in the courtyard, they showed her the fountain. "Is that it?" She asked the oldest and most diminutive nun, who had to turn her whole body in order to look at her, her neck and spine like one metal rod. That one didn't speak English, but the slight narrowing of her eyes seemed to communicate a semblance of understanding. She felt guilty for her question and for her obvious disappointment, just as she had when she stood in front of the Coliseum fifteen years before thinking it could have been bigger. The basin was small, knee-height, and maybe four feet in diameter, though beautiful, made of marble and filled with water so clear it reflected a brighter, more turquoise sky. The kind of water that immediately made everyone thirsty. They kept the tub and the empty apse behind it unpainted, a cool oatmeal that contrasted with the shocking Greek white of the wall it was built into. The line where the new paint ended was hilly and uneven, and the way the old ruins peeked out from the new coat reminded her of how, when her children would tear the first piece of wrapping paper from a present, a jagged, random shape would expose the surprise inside, and they'd pause to react before shedding the skin completely.

"Welcome to Agia Moni," the tour guide began. She hadn't seen him arrive, and the nuns had struggled to communicate that he was running late but would be there soon. Sophia was waiting on the bus, at this point in the trip, she had earned a break. The others stopped their awe-speckled murmurings to shuffle in closer, and she brushed elbows with the high school history teacher from Texas who didn't drink. They mouthed sorry to each other at the same instant.

"We start our tour in the courtyard for a number of reasons," he continued. He was short and smart looking, and he interlaced his fingers while he spoke, gesturing with the cage of fingers still intact and emoting with well-timed raises onto his toes followed by a couple bounces on his heels. It gave her the sense of restrained excitement.

"First of all, we rather like it out here." This garnered a few smirks from the modest crowd. "You can see the lovely hills of Nafplio surrounding you, not to mention the nuns' prized garden. And, of course, you can enjoy our warm and temperate climate year-round." Most of the group scanned their surroundings as he went on about the flora, tapped their travel companions on the arm, pointed out a vibrant flower or garden statue, shifted their weight and swayed their giant helium-ed heads around to look here and there. She looked him in the face, catching his eyes when they'd land on her for a couple seconds. She was listening. This is what she came for.

"And, of course, the other reason we start here is the history," the lowering of his voice recaptured a few members of the audience. "While, as you know, the monastery, the churches and buildings you see around you, were built in 1149 AD, but our history begins far before that." He took a few steps backwards towards the fountain and paused. Placing his hand on the rim of the basin, he took on the air of a storyteller, "Like most of the histories of the Mediterranean, ours begins with a myth."

She had read the story a thousand times, set in a thousand places. It was the story of purification, a story so ingrained in the human psyche it didn't take long for it to bubble up in the consciousness of countless civilizations. Water as healer, as baptism, as mikveh. The ritual of cleansing is so symbolic, it's bloomed out into a million myths, but it was this one that got to her. It had affected her when she uncovered it that day in New York, weeks after uncovering the chin, just as it did as the guide now told it.

She held onto her elbows while she listened, hugging in while tilting her chin out in curiosity. How would he write Hera? Benevolent mother? Perpetually unsatisfied wife? Jealous avenger of her philandering husband Zeus? Holy goddess of marriage and the hearth? She hated the renditions that deflated the goddess to one trait, failing to acknowledge the fleshed out, complete woman the historical texts described. Why could they not accept the contradictory, ambivalent nature of her? Why did people polarize the world so quickly, jealousy and fidelity, vengeance and holiness, love and sex?

He didn't disappoint her. He told the story of Hera and her ritual as she might wish she could tell it, filled with the intricate details of her marriage and offering multiple interpretations so that each audience member, from the enraptured ones to those taking selfies, might decide for themselves. Maybe Hera submerged herself every year at the spring of Nauplia, renewing her virginity, in order to cleanse herself of her own marital digressions. Or she became a maiden time and time again for the pleasure of her powerful husband. Perhaps it was her duty as the goddess of marriage to be deflowered every time she went to bed with him. Maybe the reason didn't matter. What mattered was the centuries of history, the ancient Greek cults taking to the shores every year, plunging the symbolic plank of wood (as proxy for a goddess which never made much sense to her) into the sea of Samos, immersing their mother goddess, *we only love you when you're clean!*, pulling her out from the waves, *a wife with a regenerative hymen!*, placing her back in the sacrum of their temple, *a woman who can stand on that impossibly thin line between virgin and slut for all eternity!*

"The water you see in this fountain is believed to be from the very spring, the spring called Kanathos, where Hera would bathe." He ran his fingers over the surface of the water, making a delicious sound. She couldn't help it, she had to ask.

"So that's it?" She didn't mean to sound so abrasive. All the eyes turned to look at her.

The first time she had seen the fountain was on her computer screen back in upstate New York. With no person in the photo, the fountain had appeared much larger. She assumed it would at least rise to her hips. Of all the places that claimed to be Kanathos, this one appealed to her the most. She felt a connection immediately with the image, this had to be the place. The long trip down the rabbit hole of the internet that had led her here, sprouted from a simple search: how to move on after your husband cheats on you. This in turn, brought her to a community support group which brought her to MindfulMama68, or "Gwen" as she would come to know her, an online therapist who encouraged her to "cleanse her aura." She was convincing. He left his bad energy inside of you, she would say. There are ways to become pure again. Gwen's advice quickly spiraled into a plea for her to find God again. Sticking firmly to her "spiritual but not religious" identity, she left the support group after just a few talks with Gwen. But that idea of somehow regaining her virginity stuck in her head for weeks. This wasn't about cleansing herself of sin, or finding God, or even becoming pure. She simply wanted to take back just one of the things her husband had taken from her.

The tour guide looked puzzled, "I'm sorry?" He held his hand up to his ear so that he could hear the rest of her question which he assumed he had missed.

"Like that's Kanathos right there?" She pointed to the basin.

A few people exchanged side glances and uncomfortable smiles. *Who was this weird woman who ran a café, had no prior interest in the classics, and was now interrupting without shame?* He managed to stifle any laughter at her stupidity. "Well, no, that water comes from the spring. The spring itself is about a kilometer from here." He pointed off in a vague direction. "The fountain, however, was built in the..."

"So are we going there?" Now the group was sufficiently uncomfortable.

She crossed her arms again, "Sorry. I was just wondering."

"That's fine, and erm, no. There is not much to see beyond a small pond and we still have loads of history to share here!" She nodded, not wanting to cause any more discomfort but failing to hide the disappointment in her face.

"But as I was saying, the fountain is from the original 12th century monastery. And," he motioned for everyone to gather around, "you're free to drink from it."

The nuns started filling ceramic cups, while he answered more questions, mostly about the current nunnery and history of the church. They had allowed the tub to fill by covering up the small drain at the bottom, and the clear water continued to flow from the narrow stone channel.

Smart. She could imagine filling the eight cups from the stream would have taken quite a while. The basin was maybe three-quarters full. She clasped the cool cup in her hands, and clinked with Patty, the sisters from Maine, the oldest members of the group.

The women made jokes about becoming pure again, returning home to their husbands in white dresses. They hung around the edge of the fountain. She chuckled and took a long gulp. It was so cool she felt the water flow down her throat and esophagus. The guide started leading the group into the church while the nuns herded close behind. She loitered at the back of the lot, no one noticing her hanging behind for a few seconds. In that brief second, she was alone with the water, she dunked her left hand up to the wrist, her fingers swirling around in the magic waters. When she pulled it out, she wiped it on the hem of her spring jacket, looked at it for a moment, and turned around. She could just make out a small path into the woods where the guide had indicated. A kilometer he had said? That wouldn't be more than a 10 minute walk. She had come all this way for one reason, and she sure as hell wasn't getting back on that plane to New York without at least trying. She took her phone out to pretend to take some final photos while the group started shuffling into the church. She had always followed all the rules. And what had that gotten her? She heard the door bounce closed and knew this was her chance, so she took off towards the woods.

Her heart pounded as she walked up the narrow path, which led up the side of a hill to a ledge. The path was short but steep, sprinkled with the kind of stones that like to shift under your weight at surprising times. She kept her phone map out so she could see she was moving towards a small blue blip that indicated water. When she got to the ledge just a few yards wide, she heard the running water. She rounded a bend and she saw the pond, a small clear pool surrounded by mossy grey stones. The smallest waterfall she had ever seen cascaded into it from one side. She could see to the bottom, maybe three feet down. She was really going to do this. This crazy idea of hers, this mission that had pulled her through the last few long months of her life, was right there in front of her. She had asked the universe to grant her this one insane desire, and here it was. She took off her clothes and sat on the edge of a frigid rock. She scooched forward and put her feet in, sliding them slowly until she could feel the slippery surface below. She stood in the cold water for a mere second before submerging herself. When she ricocheted back up, gasping from the cold, she immediately burst out laughing. Holding her own shivering body, she convulsed from the cool afternoon air and the uncontrollable laughter that consumed her. What an obsession this had been, what a ridiculous quest she had set out for herself, what a crazy, adventure-filled life she could have before her.

She used the extra cardigan in her bag to towel off, but her hair was still wet when she made her way back and rejoined the group. They were back out in the courtyard, and the tour guide was clearly offering up his closing remarks. The others had not noticed her absence, and if they did probably assumed she had taken the time to rest in the bus, sick for lunch or otherwise uninterested in another tour. The tour guide seemed to take in her wet hair and muffle out the surprise that swept across his face. He continued, "So you see there are many histories here. Like layers, some more mysterious than others.

Regardless, this site has maintained its holy nature for centuries and centuries, with evidence of cult practice dating back to the second century." With his final words, his eyes came to rest on hers, "So perhaps it's less important what happened here and when. Or if anything magical really happened here at all. But beyond that, the stories that persist, the stories we tell ourselves about ourselves over and over again, regardless of truth, they matter."

THE TOPOGRAPHY OF RUIN

Arx Tarpeia Capitoli Proxima[*1]

752 B.C. Rome is a hellscape; populated by criminals, low-lives, and outcasts, men who have killed and defiled. The city has no shame. It's hard to imagine that this is the same Rome that will become an empire, its boundaries unfurling over rivers and mountains and seas and languages. Actually, it's not hard to imagine. It's inevitable that a civilization built with no shame would light quickly and wildly, scorching across the earth like a meteor, without hesitation or limit, before crumbling to dust. They say Rome's decline began the moment Romulus sank his standard into the soil wet with his brother's blood, that a civilization fueled so hungrily by conquest without regard for the conquered is so obviously doomed to crumble. There is nothing obvious in the workings of a colonizer. He slits a people's throat, yet somehow, they become the savages. He rapes women, and they become the desecrated. Everyone he drains of power he fills with shame. His wake is eternal.

In the pre-dawn hours, Tarpeia goes to get holy water from the well outside the gates. She is one of the first Vestal Virgins, the priestesses of the hearth goddess, whose main role is to guard over the sacred fire, never allowing it to go out. She has taken her vow, 30 years of promised celibacy, and therefore she is freed of her

---

[1] The Tarpeian Rock is close to the Capitol/The steepest fall is from the top

obligation to marry and bear children. The Vestals are the few women in Rome who have not been stolen, ripped from their homelands and fathers who refused to allow marriages with the disgraceful Roman tribe. It's only been days since King Romulus, worried mighty Rome wouldn't last more than a generation, orchestrated the abduction of 30 Sabine women with his awful trick. The Sabines are livid, and payback is due. There is outrage in the air, and Tarpeia can sense the impending conflict. When she turns to see the approaching Sabine army in the distance, she is mesmerized. Even from a distance she can see the light dance off their bejeweled golden bracelets. She imagines stacking them up her arms, dripping in their brilliance. She must have them.

As the army approaches, she devises a plan. She will give them the keys to the fortress, if only they share their jewelry with her. As they come closer, their adornments become more and more exquisite, the rubies, emeralds, precious metals taking shape and calling to her. At long last, the general approaches her. She knows who he is, Titus Tatius, his gold gleams with more exuberance than the rest. "General," she calls out. "I know you have come for revenge. I will grant you the key to the city gates, if you hand over what you bear on your left arms." The Sabines agree. "Hand over the keys, and we will bestow upon you what you have asked for." He motions his troops forward while she plants the key in his palm. One by one, the soldiers keep up their end of the bargain, removing their shields, which they also bore on their left arms, and crushing the girl to death beneath the weight of her own betrayal. Despite their benefit, even the Sabines despise a traitor. When the Romans find her body, they cast her from an 80-foot cliff, a cliff that comes to be called the Tarpeian Rock, named after the first traitor to Rome and the death sentence for all who dare to follow in her path.

***

Nora and Amelia met at tryouts for the acrobatics class at their town's dance studio just before starting Kindergarten. Yes, this was the type of dance studio that makes 5-year-olds audition, sorting them into acro A and acro B, aka those destined to be real gymnasts and the rest. Their moms waited anxiously to the side, while each girl exhibited her skills: a series of poses, jumps, forward somersaults, and where applicable, cartwheels. The two girls were among the youngest of the group, so they sat next to each other and went last, assumed by the instructors to be destined for group B. Amelia went first. Nora watched her strut her way to the mat with more confidence than the older kids. She was a prodigy even then, she held her poses in an exact replica of the teenage instructor and quickly they moved her to the tumbling floor. Her cartwheels were pure magic, they seemed to move in slow motion, with an almost DaVincian precision. Nora was in awe. The whole room was, as the child was led through backbends and round-offs and even handsprings. More than anything Nora wanted to join this girl in Acro A, she was determined to become her best friend.

13 years later, Nora and Amelia are inseparable. In the mornings Nora picks Amelia up from her house across town before school. In the car rides they discuss their

future dreams, Amelia to land on a college gymnastics program and start her own gym, and Nora to become a Nobel-Prize-winning physicist. After school, they go to practice together, though their high school gymnastics team is nothing to write home about and not on any college recruitment radar. It's their only option since the dance studio ran itself out of money. A group of its former students, including Nora and Amelia, petitioned the school to start a team and raised just enough to buy off the studio's old beam, vault, and bars and purchase a few new mats. Amelia, the team captain, coaches the other girls how to land their flips and choreographs all their routines, skills she picked up and mastered from a combination of her earlier years at the dance studio, a scrambling of sub-par summer camps she afforded with babysitting money, and the sheer force of a teenager equipped with the internet and a hell of a lot of will. She even managed to find a regional competition at a high school over an hour away. She gives her best routines to herself and Nora, spending extra time helping her best friend nail every move. In return, Nora helps Amelia study. School comes as naturally to Nora as gymnastics comes to Amelia. Words and numbers untangle themselves in her mind. She racks up awards across all the subjects, but loves science the best, physics most of all, the way it provides a semblance of a system to understand how the universe works around her.

It's the fall of their senior year, and Nora has already accepted a full academic scholarship to the local college. She's already taken classes at the school through the dual degree program and can't say no to their offer for full tuition, room and board. She knows she could have gotten into a much better school, but she doesn't want to feel the guilt of her mother who wouldn't be able to afford it since her dad lost all their money and left. This way, she can help out with her younger brother who will be starting high school, and after a year or two of straight As lock in a scholarship somewhere better. Amelia is in the process of back-up applications in case she doesn't land an athletic scholarship. With Nora's help, she can easily get into the community college as well, but they don't have a gymnastics program. She agrees to apply there, but in her heart of hearts dreams of attending the University of Oklahoma, whose team has been ranked number one for as long as she can remember. She's good enough to be on the team, she knows that, Nora knows that, the whole town knows that, the trick is letting the university know that. Knowing that she won't be taken seriously unless she is seen by a coach, she convinces the school's athletic director, a man who devotes 98% of his attention and time to the school's abysmal football team, to invite the coaches to their next regional competition, which he agrees to do because all it entails is copying the draft email Nora helped her perfect and hitting send. It's a Thursday afternoon when she finds out they have agreed and are sending an assistant coach to the regional competition. The first person she tells is Nora.

On the day of the coach's visit, the girls partake in their typical pre-competition ritual. Nora drives Amelia to the mall on the outskirts of town, where the smoothie shop makes acai bowls filled with granola and berries and chocolate. They blast 80s workout music in the car and try to dance off their nerves. Amelia barely eats two bites, she can't control herself, she babbles the whole time about how this is her big break, her destiny. Everything is falling into place. Nora's heart sinks as she realizes that this might mean she will be starting the next chapter of her life without her best, and really only, friend. Beautiful, talented Amelia, who always seems to get everything she wants will be off fulfilling her dream, and where will that leave Nora? They get to the gym hours early and start warming up and primping. Nora watches her friend paint on mascara and grease her hair into a perfect bun, thinking how unfair it is that Amelia will get a state university education she doesn't even care about, while Nora will be stuck in town at the community college, alone and bored.

The competition starts, and there isn't an OU logo in sight. Nora is up first, and Amelia third. Nora performs well, gets the best scores she has ever scored across the board, and the whole team envelops her in a big hug. This is her last competition, of high school, and therefore forever, and she is flushed with the excitement of going out so strongly. The only person who doesn't congratulate her is Amelia, she is too busy panicking that the coach will miss her performance. Her stress is overwhelming, and Nora can't take it. How come it always has to be about Amelia? How come no one cared when she made Acro A as a four-year-old because Amelia did it better? Why does Amelia deserve the world? She goes outside for some air, while Amelia goes off to do some final stretches. From the corner of her eye she sees a car park across the lot, the door slams, and a man comes running toward her, clearly frazzled and not used to turning up late, asking if that's the door to the gym. She knows he is the coach. Everything about him screams university money, from the perfectly pressed slacks to the neat logo on his crimson polo. He looks more professional than any coach or teacher she's ever laid eyes on. He comes from a world of excellence, money, and worldliness. If she couldn't have this, her friend shouldn't either.

"Yes," she says. "But they are taking a break." The words tumble out her mouth.

"A break?" He says. She knows Amelia has started her floor routine, where she shines the brightest. In just 180 seconds, she will be done.

"Yes, they had to adjust something with the speakers or something. Hey, are you from OU?"

"I am," he says, reaching for the door. "I should really get in there. I was given the wrong address and am already late."

He opens the door, but she grabs his arm so quickly he doesn't get a chance to look inside where her friend stands in the corner of the mat, poised to begin, staring straight at the them. "I think you need to check in through the front entrance," she stammers out. "It's a security thing. I can walk you."

She slowly walks the scout around the parking lot, through the front doors of the school. When they make it to the gym, Amelia is already on the beam though her music hasn't begun. She can't fathom what she just saw, her best friend pulling the scout away from her big moment. The heartbreak, rage, and anxiety compound in her chest. She takes her first cartwheel, a move she has made a million times without thinking, though her arms quake with emotion her feet meet the beam. She, for the first time, is not steady on her feet and it throws her. She takes her first leap in the air, and crashes down hard, falling off the beam entirely. The coach writes her a note that comes with her rejection letter, he explains that while her videos were promising and he understands that these moments are nerve-wracking, the trait he looks for the most is the ability to perform under great pressure, reliability, consistency. She is not offered a place on the team.

When she sees Nora after the meet, she looks her dead in the eye and says, *how dare you.* The entire crowd seems to glare at her, wretched Nora who clearly couldn't take living in Amelia's shadow for another moment. Nora begins college without a friend in the world.

***

752 B.C. Tarpeia is out fetching holy water, when she sees the Sabine army flooding forth, dozens of young men, flushed with anger and the excitement of attack, driven by the mad desire to get their women back. She is rarely allowed to be around so many men, having been promised to the goddess and the fire. When she sees general Titus Tatius, she is overcome with desire. She must have him.

When he approaches her and demands she hand over the key to the gates, she laughs, "I would hand you the key," she coos, inching her body close to the dreamy general's. "But what would I get from you in return?" She looks his body up and down, taking in every inch before settling on his eyes. He reaches his palm out for the keys, and she slowly drops them in his hand, letting hers rest on top of his for a moment. In that instant he seizes her wrist, and tosses her to the ground, ordering his men to crush her to death with their shields. Despite their benefit, even the Sabines despise a slut. When the Romans find her body, they cast her from a cliff so tall it looks like she's thrown to the sky.

***

It's the day of the competition and the coach is nowhere to be seen. Nora has just come off her triumphant last performance, and she turns to her friend for congratulations. Amelia is too busy stressing. Nora can't take it. She goes outside for some air, and when she is about to turn back, she sees a car pull into the lot. The man who emerges is the most gorgeous man she has ever laid eyes on. Boys her own age have acne and facial hair that look like pubes. He is a man, with a neat, thick beard and muscles that have been developed over years. "Is this the gym?" He asks.

Her hand is on the handle to the door, but he is still just a step too far to see what's inside, to see her best friend on the mat, poised to begin. She lets the door close as he approaches. He radiates confidence, and poise, and money. The nearer he comes, the more she wants him. "Are you here for the meet?" she asks, leaning her weight on the door and blinking her eyes slowly the way she sees women do in movies.

"Ya, and I am running late so I really need to get in there." He says, stepping to the side and waiting for her to move.

"Let me walk you," Nora says eagerly, patting her hand on his chest. "We have to go in through the front."

She walks slowly and seductively, while he does his best to rush her. When they enter the gym, she sits on the bleachers, and pats the seat next to her with a wink. The scout brushes past her and joins the coaches' table.

Amelia sees her friend from the beam, Nora, her boy-crazy, slutty best friend, is drooling over the handsome scout and distracting him from her big moment. She is filled with such rage she can hardly focus. She leaps, she falls.

When she sees Nora after the meet, she looks her dead in the eye and says, *how dare you.* Nora begins college without a friend in the world.

***

752 B.C. Tarpeia turns too late. She drops the holy water, and begins to run to warn the others, but the army is on her and surrounded her before she can blink.

"Well if it isn't one of their little priestesses," The general titters. The soldiers laugh. "Should we do to her what they did to our women?" They guffaw, close in on her.

"Please," she begs, mustering whatever ounce of bravery she can find. "Please, put down your weapons!"

"You heard the girl," the general snickers. "Put down your weapons." A wicked smile spills across his face.

When the Romans find her body crushed beneath all the shields, they toss her to the depths of hell.

***

The competition has begun, and the scout is nowhere to be seen. Nora races through her own routine, nervous for her friend whose whole future is riding on the next few minutes. Apparently, overthinking on behalf of her friend serves her well, she gets the best scores she has ever received, but doesn't even notice. She runs back to Amelia to assure it will be OK, he will show up. While her friend goes to stretch, she takes matters into her own hands, figuring the coach probably got lost.

She goes into the parking lot to try and call the number he included in the confirmation letter. As she goes out into the fall air, she sees a car pull into the lot and waves it down. It's him. In all of her excitement, she moves her foot from the door, and it closes behind her. She lunges for it, but it's too late. They are locked out and will have to go around the whole building. She rushes him to the gym, telling him how amazing her friend is, how she deserves a spot on his team more than anyone.

When they reach the gym, Amelia is already on the beam. She sees her friend run into the gym with the one person who could have changed her destiny. She knows it is somehow all Nora's fault. She leaps. She falls what feels like 80 feet. Even after the million times Nora explains, she can't look at her friend again. Theirs was a friendship built on dreams.

***

752 B.C. An army of men descends on Rome, enraged at the city for its crimes against their women. They raze the city gates and trample everything in their path, including a young priestess who never saw them coming.

Acknowledgments

Thank you to my mentors and thesis committee at the University of Massachusetts, Amherst's MFA for Poets & Writers including Sabina Murray, Mona Awad, and Edie Meidav. Your guidance throughout workshops helped me crystallize my mission as a fiction writer to revitalize ancient myths and explore the intricacies with which they echo throughout our daily lives. Thank you to the many readers who wrestled with these stories both in and out of workshop with me, a special thanks to my Lighthouse Workshop companion, Carly Schmidt, whose wise feedback was a beacon and inspiration during the chaos of the editing process, my Graves Street neighbor and dear friend, Roxanne Ringer, and friends Kathryn Sullivan, Olivia Barry, Andrea Marshall, and Ana Cvetković for your thoughtful input. To my dad, sister, husband, and son— thank you for your constant support and love. And most of all, to my mom, thank you for sitting with me always, through all the seasons and storms.

THE AUTHOR

Emily Marcus Gong is a writer and educator located in Boston, MA. She earned her BA in Classical Studies from The George Washington University and is a 2021 graduate of UMass Amherst's MFA for Poets & Writers with a focus on fiction. Her freelance lifestyle and travel writing can be found in numerous regional and national publications including *Connect Corporate Magazine*, *World Bride Magazine, kimkim.com, Hey Alma*, and *New England Living*, among others. Her poetry and short fiction appears in *Eunoia Review, Red Noise Collective, Right Hand Pointing*, and the Australian Writers' Centre. Emily currently serves as an Academic Advisor and PT Writing Lecturer at Northeastern University.

Find her at emilymarcusgong.com

www.ingramcontent.com/pod-product-compliance
Lightning Source LLC
Chambersburg PA
CBHW020048310726
48970CB00007B/2459